100 Reasons to Celebrate

We invite you to join us in celebrating
Mills & Boon's centenary. Gerald Mills and
Charles Boon founded Mills & Boon Limited
in 1908 and opened offices in London's Covent
Garden. Since then, Mills & Boon has become
a hallmark for romantic fiction, recognised
around the world.

We're proud of our 100 years of publishing
excellence, which wouldn't have been achieved
without the loyalty and enthusiasm of our
authors and readers.

Thank you!

Each month throughout the year there will
be something new and exciting to mark the
centenary, so watch for your favourite authors,
captivating new stories, special limited
edition collections…and more!

Dear Reader

When I started writing, eight years ago, I never imagined that my stories would find their way to Mills & Boon: the birthplace of the modern romance novel. It is a source of great pride to know that my 'imaginary friends' are in the care of a company whose history stretches halfway back to the Regency.

I hope you enjoy my story of Constance Townley, a lonely widow who is about to meet the man who will spoil her plans for a respectable remarriage. But how can she settle for a life without passion after Tony Smythe steals her heart?

Of course I've grown quite fond of both Tony and Constance, who have been my close companions for several months. They are quite an exciting pair. When I sat down to write their story, I was never sure if I would be waltzing at Vauxhall or climbing into windows and picking imaginary locks. And together they do indeed have some wicked liaisons, and manage to live happily ever after, following in the footsteps of one hundred years of Mills & Boon® characters.

Happy reading

And Happy Anniversary, Mills & Boon!

Christine

A WICKED LIAISON

Christine Merrill

MILLS & BOON
Pure reading pleasure

First published in Great Britain 2007
Paperback edition 2008
Harlequin Mills & Boon Limited,
Eton House, 18-24 Paradise Road, Richmond, Surrey TW9 1SR

© Christine Merrill 2007

ISBN: 978 0 263 86237 9

Set in Times Roman 10¾ on 13¾ pt.
04-0108-72634

Printed and bound in Spain
by Litografia Rosés S.A., Barcelona

To Maddie Rowe, editor extraordinaire.

You make this so much fun
that I forget I'm working.

Christine Merrill lives on a farm in Wisconsin, USA, with her husband, two sons, and too many pets—all of whom would like her to get off the computer so they can check their e-mail. She has worked by turns in theatre costuming, where she was paid to play with period ballgowns, and as a librarian, where she spent the day surrounded by books. Writing historical romance combines her love of good stories and fancy dress with her ability to stare out of the window and make stuff up.

Recent novels by the same author:

THE INCONVENIENT DUCHESS
AN UNLADYLIKE OFFER

Chapter One

Anthony de Portnay Smythe sat at his regular table in the darkest corner of the Blade and Scabbard pub. The grey wool of his coat blended with the shadows around him, rendering him almost invisible to the rest of the room. Without appearing to—for to stare at his fellows might prove suicidally rude—he could observe the other patrons. Cutpurses, thieves, petty criminals and transporters of stolen goods. Rogues to a man. And, for all he knew, killers.

Of course, he took great care not to know.

The usual feelings of being comfortable and in his element were unusually disconcerting. He dropped a good week's work on to the table and pushed them towards his old friend, Edgar.

Business associate, he reminded himself. Although they had known each other for many years, it would be a mistake to call his relationship with Edgar a friendship.

'Rubies.' Tony sorted through the gems with his finger, making them sparkle in the light of the candle guttering on the table. 'Loose stones. Easy to fence. You need not even pry them from the settings. The work has been done for you.'

'Dross,' Edgar countered. 'I can see from here the stones are flawed. Fifty for the lot.'

This was where Tony was supposed to point out that they were investment-grade stones, stolen from the study of a marquis. The man had been a poor judge of character, but an excellent judge of jewellery. Then Tony would counter with a hundred and Edgar would try to talk him down.

But suddenly, he was tired of the whole thing. He pushed the stones further across the table. 'Fifty it is.'

Edgar looked at him in suspicion. 'Fifty? What do you know that I do not?'

'More than I can tell you in an evening, Edgar. Far more. But I know nothing about the stones that need concern you. Now give me the money.'

This was not how the game was to be played. And thus, Edgar refused to acknowledge that he had won. 'Sixty, then.'

'Very well. Sixty.' Tony smiled and held out his hand for the money.

Edgar narrowed his eyes and stared at Tony, trying to read the truth. 'You surrender too easily.'

It felt like a long hard fight on Tony's side of the table. Tonight's dealings were just a skirmish at the end of the war. He sighed. 'Must I bargain? Very well, then. Seventy-five and not a penny less.'

'I could not offer more than seventy.'

'Done.' Before the fence could speak again, he forced the stones into Edgar's hand and held his other hand out for the purse.

Edgar seemed satisfied, if not exactly happy. He accepted the stones and moved away from the table, disappearing into the haze of tobacco smoke and shadows around them, and Tony went back to his drink.

As he sipped his whisky, he reached into his pocket to remove the letter and his reading glasses. He absently polished the spectacles on his lapel before putting them on, then settled his chin in his hands to read.

Dear Uncle Anthony,

We are so sorry that you were unable to attend the wedding. Your gift was more than generous, but it does not make up in my heart for your absence on my most happy of days. I hardly know what to say in thanks for this and so many other things you have done for my mother and me over the years. Since Father's death, you have been like a second father to me, and my cousins say the same.

It was good to see Mother finally marry again, and I am happy that Mr Wilson could be there to walk me down the aisle, but I cannot help but think you deserved the position more than he. I do not wish my marriage or my mother's to estrange me from your company, for I will always value your wise counsel and your friendship.

My husband and I will welcome your visit, as soon as you are able.

Your loving niece, Jane

Tony stopped to offer a prayer of thanks for the presence of Mr Wilson. His sister-in-law's discovery of Mr Wilson, and marriage to same, had stopped in its tracks any design she might have had to see Tony standing at the altar in a capacity other than loving brother or proud uncle.

Marriage to one of his brothers' widows might have been expedient, since he had wished to involve himself financially and emotionally in the raising of their children, but the idea always left him feeling squeamish. Not an emotion he sought, when viewing matrimony. Seeing the widows of his two elder brothers well married, in a way that did not leave him legshackled to either of them, had been a load off his troubled brow.

And the wedding of young Jane was another happy incident, whether he could be there to attend or no. With the two widows and only niece comfortably remarried, all to gentlemen that met his approval, he had but to worry about the boys.

And, truth be told, there was little to worry about from either of his nephews, the young earl or his brother. Both were settled at Oxford, with their tuitions paid in full for the duration of their stay. The boys were sensible and intelligent, and appeared to be growing into just the sort of men that he could wish for.

And it left Tony—he looked at the letter in front of him. It left him extraneous. He had hoped, when at last he saw the family set to rights, to feel a rush of elation. He was free of responsibility and the sole master of his own life. Now that the time had come, it was without joy.

With no one to watch over, just what was he to do with his time? Over the years, he had invested wisely for the family as well as for himself, and his forays into crime had been less and less necessary and more a relief from the boredom of respectability.

Now that he lacked the excuse that there were mouths to feed and no money in the bank, he must examine his motivations and face the fact that he was no better than the common criminals around him. He had no reason to steal, save the need to feel the life coursing through him when he hung by drainpipes and window sills, fearing detection, disgrace or, worst of all, incarceration, and knowing every move could be his last.

No reason save one, he reminded himself. There

was a slight movement in the heavy air as the door to the tavern opened and St John Radwell, Earl of Stanton, entered and strode purposefully towards the table.

Tony slipped the letter back into his pocket and tried not to appear too eager to have employment. 'You are late.' He raised his glass to the earl in a mocking salute.

'Correction. You are early. I am on time.' Stanton clapped Tony on the shoulder, took the seat that Edgar had vacated, and signalled the barman for a whisky. St John's smile was mocking, but held the warmth of friendship that was absent from others Tony typically met while doing business.

'How are things in the War Department?'

'Not so messy as they were on the battlefield, thank the Lord,' responded St John. 'But still not as well as they could be.'

'You have need of my services?' Tony had no wish to let the man see how much he needed the work, but he itched to do something to take away the feeling of unease he experienced as he read the letter. Anything which might make him feel needed again.

'I do indeed. Lucky for you, and most unlucky for England. We have another bad one. Lord Barton, known to his companions as Jack. He's been a naughty boy, has Jack. He has friends in high places, and is not afraid to use those connections to get ahead.'

'Dealing with the French?' Anthony tried not to yawn.

St John grinned. 'Better than that. Jack is no garden-variety traitor. He prefers to keep his crimes within the country. Recently, a young gentleman from the Treasury Department, while in his cups and gaming in the company of Lord Barton, managed to lose a surprising amount of money very quickly. Young men often do, when playing with Barton.'

'Does he cheat?' Tony asked.

'I doubt he would balk at it, but that is not why the Treasury Department needs your help. The clerk's efforts to win back what he had lost went as well as could be expected. He continued to gamble and lost even more. Soon he was facing utter ruin. Lord Barton applied pressure and convinced the man to debase himself further still, to clear his debt. He delivered to Barton a set of engraving plates for the ten-pound note. They were flawed and going to be destroyed, but they are near enough to perfect to make the notes almost undetectable.'

'Counterfeiting?' Tony could not but help admire the audacity of the man, even as he longed to ruin his plans.

St John nodded. 'The clerk regretted his act almost immediately, but it was too late. Barton is now in a perfect position to destabilise the currency for his own benefit.'

'And you need me to steal your plates back.'

'You will be searching his home for an excessive number of ten-pound notes, paper, inks and, most especially, those plates. Use your discretion. Your utmost discretion, actually. This must not become a public scandal, but it must end immediately, before he begins circulating the money. We wish to break him quickly and quietly, so as not to upset the banks or the exchange.'

The earl dropped a full purse on the table. 'As usual, half in advance and half when the job is completed. Feel free to take an additional payment from the personal wealth of Barton and any associates you might need to search. He has homes in London and Essex. But it has been less than a week since the theft. I doubt he has had time to get the plates out of the city.' As an afterthought, Stanton added, 'You had best search his mistress's home, as well.'

'A criminal's mistress?' Tony grinned. 'You are sending me off to search the perfumed boudoir of some notorious courtesan? And paying me for the privilege.' He rolled his eyes. 'I fear what may become of me, if I am discovered by her. I had no idea that government service would hold such hardship.'

St John sighed with mock-aggravation. 'I doubt there will be any such threat to your dubious virtue, Smythe. The lady is of good character, or was until Barton got his hooks into her. The widow of a peer. It is a shame to see such an attractive young thing consort with the likes of Jack. But one never knows.' He scrawled an address down on a scrap of paper. 'Her Grace, the Dowager Duchess of Wellford. Constance Townley.'

Tony felt the earth lurch under him, as it always did when her name rose unexpectedly in a conversation. But this time, it was compounded by a thrill of horror at hearing it in the current context.

Oh, my God, Connie. What has become of you?

He took a careful swallow of the whisky before speaking. Any hoarseness in his voice could be attributed to the harsh spirit in his glass. 'The loveliest woman in London.'

'So they say,' St John responded. 'The second-loveliest, perhaps. She is a particular friend of my wife and I've often had the opportunity to compare them.'

'Night and day,' remarked Tony, thinking of Constance's shining black hair, her huge dark eyes, her pale skin, next to the fair beauty of Esme Radwell. In his mind, there was no comparison. But to be polite he said, 'You are a fortunate man.'

'As well I know.'

'And you say the duchess has become Barton's mistress.'

'So I have been told. It is likely to become most awkward in my home, for I cannot very well encourage Esme to associate with her, if the rumours are true. But Constance is often seen in Barton's company and he is most adamant about his intentions towards her in conversation with others. Either she is his, or soon will be.'

Tony shook his head in pretended sympathy, along

with Stanton, and said, 'A shame, indeed. But at least that part of the search will be of no difficulty. If the duchess is naïve enough to involve herself with Barton, then she might be unprepared to prevent my search and careless in hiding her part in the crime. When would you like results?'

'As soon as can be managed safely.'

Tony nodded. 'I will begin tonight. With Constance Townley, for she will be the weak link, if there is one. And you will hear from me as soon as I have something to tell.'

Stanton nodded in return. 'I will leave you to it, then. As usual, do not fail me, and do not get caught. My wife expects you to dinner on Thursday and it will be damned difficult explaining to her if you cannot attend because I have got you arrested.' He stood then, and took his leave, disappearing into the crowd and out the door.

Tony stared down into his glass and ignored the pounding blood in his ears. What was he to do about Constance? He had imagined her lying alone in the year following her husband's death, and expected she would be quietly remarried to some honourable man soon after her period of mourning ended.

But to take up with Barton, instead? The thought was repellent. The man was a cad as well as a criminal. Handsome, of course. And well mannered to ladies. He appeared most personable, if you did not know the truth of his character.

But at thirty, Constance was no green girl to be dazzled by good looks and false charm. She might appear to be nothing more than a beautiful ornament, but Tony remembered the sharp mind behind the beauty. Even when she was a girl, she would never have been so foolish as to fall for the likes of Jack Barton. And the thought that she would willingly betray her own country…

He shook his head. He could not bring himself to believe it. If he must search her for Stanton, best to do it quickly and know the truth. And to do so, he must put the past behind him and clear his mind for the night's work ahead of him. He finished the whisky, dropped a sovereign on the table for the barman, and went off into the night, to satisfy his curiosity as to the morals of the Dowager Duchess of Wellford.

Chapter Two

Tony did not need to refer to Stanton's directions—he knew well the location of the house in London where the dowager resided. He'd walked by it often enough in daylight for the twelve months that she'd been in residence. Without intending to observe the place, he'd given himself a good idea of the layout of rooms by watching the activities in the windows as he passed.

Her bedroom would be at the back of the house, facing a small garden. And there would be an alleyway for tradesmen somewhere about. He'd never seen a delivery to the front door.

He worked his way down the row of townhouses, to a cross street and a back alley, counting in reverse until he could see the yellow brick of the Wellford house. As he went, he pulled a dark scarf from his pocket and wrapped it around his neck to hide the white of his shirtfront. His coat and breeches were dark, and needed no cover. Greys, blacks, and dark blues suited him well and blended with the shadows as he needed them to.

The wrought-iron gate was locked, but he found an easy toe-hold in the garden wall beside it. He swung himself to the top with no difficulty, crouching in the protection of a tree. Then, he gauged the distance of open ground to the house. Four paces to the rose-bush, another two to the edge of the terrace and up the ivy trellis at the corner of the house. And, please God, let it hold his weight, for the three storeys to the bedroom window would be no problem to climb, but damned tricky should he fall.

He was across the yard and up the ivy in a flash, happy to find the trellis anchored to the brickwork with stout bolts, and a narrow ledge beneath the third-storey window sill. He walked along it in the darkness, feet sure as though he was walking down a city street.

He stopped when he reached the window he suspected was hers. If it had been his house, he would have chosen another room for solitude, but this one had the best view of the garden. When he had known her, she had enjoyed flowers and he'd been told that the gardens at the Wellford manor had been most splendid because of the duchess's attentions. If she wished to see the rose-bushes, she would choose this room.

He slipped a penknife under the frame, feeling along until he found the latch and felt it slide open with the pressure of the blade. Then he raised the sash a few inches, and listened at the gap.

There were no candles lit. The room was dark and quiet. He threw the window the rest of the way open, and listened again for an oath, an exclamation, anything that might indicate he had been heard. When nothing came, he stepped through the window and stood for a moment behind the curtain, letting his eyes adjust to the dim glow from the banked coals in the grate.

He was alone. He stepped further into the room, and was shocked to feel a wave of sadness and longing overtake him.

So it was not to be as easy as he'd hoped. The irrational jealousy he'd felt, when he'd heard she had found a protector so soon after leaving off her mourning, was burning away. He had hoped he could keep the anger fresh, and use it to protect his resolve when the time came to search her rooms. If she was no longer the innocent girl he remembered, but instead a traitorous whore, then she deserved punishment.

But he probed his heart and knew vengeance would be impossible, as would justice. If there was something to find in the room, he would find it.

And he would destroy it before St John Radwell and the government could ever see. He could not let Barton continue, but he would not let Constance be punished for her lover's crimes. If there was a way to bring her out of it with a whole skin, he would do it, no matter the cost to his own reputation.

He scanned the room. He had chosen well. It was definitely a lady's bedroom: large and high-ceilinged, decorated in rose with delicate furniture. Along the far wall, there was a soft and spacious bed.

Where the Duchess of Wellford entertained Jack Barton.

He turned away from it, looking anywhere but towards the bed.

He had expected to find a well-appointed boudoir, but this room was strangely empty. It was pretty enough, but almost monastic in its simplicity. On the walls there was no decoration. He ran his hands along the floral paper and felt for empty hooks. There should be sconces, there and there. And in the centre? A painting, perhaps, or a mirror with a gilt frame.

He strode across the room, to the wardrobe, threw open the doors, and was momentarily stunned by the scent of her. He closed his eyes and inhaled. Lavender. Had she always smelled this sweet? It had been so many years...

Eyes still shut, he navigated by touch through the dark wardrobe, his fingers playing along the back panels and feeling no spaces, no concealed latches. He patted the gowns and cloaks, feeling for lumps in pockets and finding none.

He opened his eyes again and went through the drawers, one at a time, feeling no false bottoms, nothing concealed between the dainties folded there. Silk and linen and fine Indian cotton. Things that had touched her body more intimately than he ever would. His fingers closed on a handkerchief, edged in lace and embroidered with a C. Impulsively, he took it and thrust it into his pocket, moving to the dresser to continue his search.

The Dowager Duchess of Wellford perched on the edge of her seat in her parlour, staring hopefully at the man on the couch next to her.

He was about to speak.

It was about time. He had been hinting for weeks.

She did her best to drum up a thrill of anticipation.

'Constance, there is something I wish to speak to you about.'

'Yes, Jeremy.' Jeremy Manders was not her ideal, of course, but neither had her late husband been, and they had suited well enough.

'We have known each other for a long time, since well before your husband passed. And I have always held you in high esteem.'

She smiled and nodded encouragement. 'And I you. You were Robert's good friend, and mine.'

'But I will admit, even while Robert was alive, feeling the occasional touch of envy at his good fortune in having you, Constance.'

She blushed and averted her eyes.

'I would never have dared say anything, of course, for Robert was my friend.'

She looked up again, still smiling. 'Of course not.' Her late husband, Robert, was far too much in the conversation for her taste.

'But you were quite the loveliest...still are, I mean, the loveliest woman of my acquaintance.'

'Thank you, Jeremy.' This was much better. She accepted the compliment graciously. But she wished that, just once, a man could comment on something other than her appearance.

'I hesitated to say anything, while you were still in mourning. It would hardly have been respectful.'

'Of course not.' He was hesitating to say it now, as well. Why could he not just go down on a knee and speak the words?

'But I think sufficient time has passed. And you do not appear to be otherwise engaged. I mean, you are not, are you?'

'No. My affections are not held by another, and I am quite out of my widow's weeds.' And growing older by the minute. Was it too much to expect him to seize and kiss her? That would make the point clear enough.

And it might be most romantic. But it would be too much to ask, and she forced herself not to wish for it.

'So there is no one else? Well, that is good to know.' He sagged with relief. 'I thought, if you were free, that we might do well together. You find me attractive, I hope.'

'Oh, yes, Jeremy.' She hoped it was not too obvious to a casual observer that she was reaching the point where she would find any man kind enough to offer marriage to be of surpassing handsomeness.

'And I assure you, I will be able to meet your expenses. I have ample resources, although I am not a duke, as your late husband was.'

Robert again. But Jeremy could afford to pay her bills, so let him talk. 'That is a great comfort to me.'

'And I would want you to get whatever gowns and frippery you might wish, as soon as possible. It must be most tiring to you to have to wear black for a year, and then to make do with what you had before.'

Shopping for things she did not need. She had quite forgotten what it was like. She smiled, but assured him, 'Really, it is only foolishness. It does not matter so much.'

'Oh, but it does to me. I wish to see you as bright and happy as ever you were.'

Relief flooded through her.

'I will provide a house, of course. Near Vauxhall, so that we might go there of an evening. And a generous allowance.'

'House?' The flood of relief became tainted with a trickle of doubt.

'Yes. And the dresses, of course. You could keep a staff, of…' he calculated '…three.'

'Three?'

'And your maid as well,' he amended. 'Which would really be four.'

'Jeremy, we are not negotiating my living arrangements.'

'Of course not. Any number you choose. I want you to be comfortable. And I brought with me a token of my esteem.' He reached into his pocket, and produced not a small square box, but one that was thin and slender.

She took it from him and snapped it open. 'You got me a bracelet?'

It was his turn to blush. 'There were matching earbobs. I could have got those as well, but perhaps after you say yes…'

'Jeremy, it sounds almost as though you are offering me a *carte blanche*.' She laughed a trifle too loudly at the ridiculousness of the idea.

She waited for him to laugh in return and say she was mistaken.

And he was silent.

She snapped the box shut again and thrust it back to him. 'Take it.'

'You do not like it? Because I can get another.'

'I do not want another. I do not want this one.' She could feel the colour in her face turning to an angry flush as her voice rose. 'You come here, talking of esteem, and your great fondness for me, then you offer to put me up and pay my expenses?'

Jeremy stiffened, a picture of offended dignity. 'Well, someone must, Constance. You cannot go on much longer living on your own. And surely, after twelve years of marriage, and over a year alone, you must miss the affections of a man.'

'Oh, must I?' she said through clenched teeth. 'I do not miss them so much that I seek to dishonour myself outside of marriage just to pay my bills. I thought, if you held me in such high esteem…'

'Well…' he swallowed '…here's the rub. Father will be wanting me to guarantee the inheritance. Now it's a long time before I need to worry about such. But when it comes time for me to marry, I will have to pick someone—' he searched for the correct words and finished '—that my father approves of.'

'And he will not approve of a thirty-year-old childless widow. That's what you're saying, isn't it, but you lack the spine to say it out loud? You wish to bounce me between the sheets and parade me around Vauxhall in shiny new clothes. But when it is time for you to marry, you will go to Almack's for a wide-hipped virgin.'

Jeremy squirmed in his chair. 'When you say it that way, it sounds so—'

'Accurate? Candid? Cruel? It sounds cruel because

it is, Jeremy. Now take your compliments and your jewellery and your offers of help and get them from my house.'

Jeremy drew himself up and gathered what righteousness he could. 'Your house? For how long, Constance? It is apparent to those who know you well that you are in over your head, even if you do not wish to admit it. I only meant to help you in a way that might be advantageous to both of us. And I am sure there are women who will not find what I'm suggesting so repugnant.'

There was that tone again. She had heard it before, when she'd refused such offers in the past. Reminding her not to be too particular, or to expect more than she deserved, but to settle for what was offered and be glad of it. She glared at him in silence and pointed to the door.

He rose. 'Very well. If you change your mind on the subject, send a message to my rooms. I will wait, for a time. But not for long, Constance. Do not think on it overlong. And if you expect a better offer from Barton, then you are sadly mistaken. You'll find soon enough that his friendship is no truer than mine. Good evening.'

He strode from the room, then she heard him in the hall calling for his hat and stick, and the adamant snap as the front door closed behind him.

She sat, staring into the fire, her mind racing. Jeremy was to have been the answer to all her problems.

She had been so sure of it. She had been willing to overlook a certain weakness of chin and of character. She had laughed at his boring stories. She had listened to him talk politics, and nodded, even though she could not find it in herself to agree. And she had found him foolish, sober or in mirth. She had been more than willing to marry a buffoon, and smile and nod through the rest of her life, in exchange for a little security and consistent companionship.

Maybe Jeremy had been a fool, but an honest and good-hearted one, despite his offer. And he had been right when he'd hinted that anything was better than what Lord Barton might suggest, if she allowed him to speak to her again. Jeremy could at least pretend that what he was doing would be best for both of them. There had never been any indication, when she'd looked into Jack Barton's eyes, that he cared in the slightest about anyone but himself.

'Your Grace, can I get you anything?' It was her maid, Susan, come downstairs to see what was the matter.

Constance glanced up at the clock. An hour had passed since Jeremy had gone, and she had let it, without moving from the spot. 'No, I am all right. I think I will put myself to bed this evening, Susan. Rest yourself. I will see you in the morning.'

The girl looked worried, but left her in peace.

When Constance went to stand, it felt as if she had to gather strength from deep within for the minor effort of rising from the chair. She climbed the stairs with difficulty, glad that the maid was so easily persuaded. It would be better to crawl up the stairs alone on her hands and knees than to admit how hard a blow Jeremy had struck with his non-proposal.

Susan knew the trouble she faced. The girl had found her before when she'd come to wake her, still dressed and dozing in a bedroom chair. Constance had been poring over the accounts in the wee hours, finding no way to make the expenses match the meagre allowance she received from her husband's nephew, Freddy. If only her husband had taken him in hand and taught him what would be expected, Freddy might have made a decent peer.

But Robert had been so set on the idea that they would have a child. There would be an heir, if not this year, then certainly the next. And if his own son were to inherit the title, he might never need bother with his tiresome nephew.

And now Robert was gone, and the new duke was heedless of anything but his own pleasure. He knew little of what it took to run his own estates and even less what Robert might have expected of him in regards to the welfare of the dowager.

Dowager. How she loathed the word. It always brought to mind a particularly unattractive piece of furniture. The sort of thing one put in a seldom-used room, allowing the upholstery to become faded and moth-eaten, until it was totally forgotten.

An accurate enough description, when one thought of it. Her own upholstery was sadly in need of replacement, but with the butcher's bill and the greengrocer, and the cost of coal, she dare not spend foolishly.

Of course, she could always sell the house and move to smaller accommodations, if she had the deed in hand. She had seen it, the day her husband had drawn it up. The house and its contents were clearly in her name, and he had assured her that she would not want, when his time came.

Then he had locked it in his safe and forgotten it. And now, the new duke could not be troubled to give it to her. When she asked, it was always tomorrow, or soon. She felt her lip quaver and bit it to stop the trembling. She had been a fool not to remove the keys from her husband's pocket, while his body was barely cold. She could have gone to the safe and got the deed herself and no one need have been the wiser. Now the keys and the safe belonged to Freddy and she must wait upon him to do the right thing.

Which was easier than waiting upon her suitors to offer something other than their false protection. She had been angry the first time someone had suggested that she solve her financial problems on her back. When it had happened again, anger had faded to dread. And now, it had happened so many times that she wanted nothing more than to hide in her rooms and weep.

Was this the true measure of her worth? Men admired her face and wanted her body, there was no question of that. And they seemed to enjoy her company. But never so much that they could overlook a barren womb when it came time to wed. They wanted the best of both worlds: a wife at home, great with child, and an infertile mistress tucked away for entertainment so that they could remain conveniently bastardless.

Damn Jeremy and his empty promises. She had been so sure that his hints about the future were honourable.

What was she to do now, other than to take the offer, of course? It would solve all her worries if she was willing to bend the last little bit, and give up on the idea that she could ever succeed in finding another husband. She shut the door behind her and snuffed her candle, letting the tears flow down her cheeks in the dark.

And in a corner of the room there was movement.

She caught her breath and held it. It was not a settling of the house, or a mouse in the wainscoting. That had been the scrape of a boot on the wood floor near the dresser. And then something fell from the dresser top. Her jewellery box. She could hear the meagre contents landing like hailstones on the rug.

A thief. Come to take what little she had left.

Her fatigue fled. A scream would be useless. With all the servants safely below stairs, no one would hear her. To get to the bell pull, she would need to go closer to the thief, and he would never allow her to reach it. She turned to run.

The stranger was across the room and caught her before she could move, and a hand clamped down over her mouth.

Chapter Three

'Remain silent, your Grace, and I will do what I came for and be gone. You are in no danger from me, as long as you are quiet.'

His hand eased away from her lips, but he held her close in a most familiar way, one hand at the back of her neck, the other cupping her hip, and his legs bumping against the length of her.

And suddenly, she was sick and tired of men trying to sample the merchandise without buying, or wanting to rob her, or dying and leaving her penniless and alone. She fought to free her arms and stuck him hard in the face. 'I'll give you silence, you thieving bastard.' She hit him again, in the shoulder, but his hands did not move. 'Is that quiet enough for you, you dirty sneak?' And she beat upon him with her closed fists, as silently as possible, shoulders shaking with effort, gasping out tears of rage.

He took the rain of blows in silence as well, except for the occasional grunt when a well-landed punch caused him to expel a puff of air. And when her blows began to weaken he effortlessly caught her wrists and pinned them behind her. 'Stop it, now, before you hurt yourself. You'll bruise your hands, and do more damage to them than you might to me.'

She struggled in his grip, but he held firm until the last of the fight was gone from her and there was nothing left but tears.

'Finished? Good. Now, tell me what is the trouble.' He produced a handkerchief from his pocket and offered it to her, and she was appalled to recognise it as her own.

'Trouble? Are you daft in the head? There is a man in my room, holding me against my will. And going through my lingerie.' She crushed the linen square in her hand and tossed it at his feet.

'Before that.' She could barely make out his face in the embers from the banked fire, but there was sympathy in his voice. 'You were crying before you ever knew I was here. Truth, now. What was the matter?'

'Why do you care?'

'Is it not enough to know that I do?'

'No. You have a reason for it, and as a common thief, you must wish the knowledge to use against me in some way.'

He laughed, soft in her ear. 'I am a most uncommon

thief then, for I have your interests in mind. Does it help you to trust me, if I assure you that I am a gentleman? If you met me under better circumstances, you'd find me a picture of moral fortitude. I do not drink to excess, I do not gamble, I am kind to children and animals, and I have loved only one woman the whole of my life.'

She struggled in his arms. 'And yet you do not shirk at sneaking into other women's bedrooms and taking their things.'

He sighed, but did not let her go. 'Sometimes, perhaps. But I cannot bear to see a woman in distress, and I do not steal from those that cannot afford to lose. In the box on your dresser there is a single strand of pearls and a pair of gold earrings. The rest is paste. Where is the real jewellery, your Grace?'

'Gone. Sold to pay my bills, as was much of the household furniture. You see what is there. Take it. Would you like the candlesticks from the mantel as well? They are all I have left of value. Take them and finish me.'

His grip upon her loosened, and he took her hand and bowed over it. 'I beg your pardon, your Grace. I mistook the situation. Things are not as they appear to the outside, are they? The world assumes that your husband's wealth left you financially secure.'

She gathered her dignity around her. 'I make sure of that.'

'Can you not appeal to friends for help?'

She tossed her head. 'I find, when one has no husband to defend one's honour, or family to return to, that there are not as many true friends as one might think. There are many who would prey upon a woman alone, if she shows weakness.'

'But I am not one of them.' He was still holding her hand in his and his grip was sure and warm. She thought, in the dimness, she could see a smile playing at the corners of his lips. 'I have taken nothing from your jewel case. I swear on it. And the handkerchief?' He shook his head. 'I do not know what possessed me. I am not in the habit of rifling through women's linens and taking trophies. It was a momentary aberration. I apologise and assure you that you will find nothing else missing from your personal items.'

She thought, for just a moment, how nice it would be to believe him and to think there was one man on the planet who did not mean to take more than she wished to give. 'So you have broken into my rooms and mean to take nothing, then?' she asked suspiciously.

Now she was sure she could hear the smile in his voice. 'A trifle, perhaps. Only this.' And he pulled her close again to bring her mouth to his.

The thief did not bother with the niceties. There was no gentle caress, no hesitation, no request for permission. He opened her mouth and he took.

She steeled herself against the violation, deciding,

if it was a choice of the two, she had much rather he took a kiss than the candlesticks. It was foolish of her to have mentioned them, for she needed the money their sale would bring.

In any case, at least the kiss would be over soon and she did not need to spare his feelings and pretend passion where she felt none, as she had with Jeremy. But unlike Jeremy, this man was most expert at kissing.

Her mind drifted. His hand was on her shoulder and her head rested in the crook of his elbow, as he tipped her back in the cradle of his arms. It felt strangely comforting to be held by the stranger. She need barely support herself, for he was doing a most effective job of bearing her weight. She tilted her head slightly, and he adjusted, tasting her lips and her tongue as though he wanted to have every last bit of sweetness from them before letting her go.

She relaxed and gave it up to him. And was shocked to find herself willing to give him more. It had been a long time since she had felt so well and truly kissed. Her husband's kisses, in recent years, had been warm and comfortable, but not particularly passionate. The kisses she'd received from suitors since his death were more ardent, but could not seem to melt the frozen places in her heart, or ease the loneliness.

But this man kissed as if he were savouring a fine wine. He was dallying with her, barely touching her lips and then sealing their mouths to steal the breath from her lungs.

His hands were gentle on her body, taking no further liberty than to support her as he kissed, and she knew she had but to offer the slightest resistance and he would set her free.

But she was so tired of being free, if freedom meant loneliness and worry. And suddenly, the kiss could not be long enough or deep enough to satisfy the craving inside of her. His hands stayed still on her body, but she wished to feel them do more than just hold her. She wanted to be touched.

Her own hands were clenched in fists on his shirtfront, and she realised that she'd planned to push him away before now. Instead she opened them, palms flat and fingers spread on his chest, before running them up his body to wrap her arms around his neck. The hair at the back of his head was soft, and curled around her fingers as she tangled them in it, pulling herself closer to kiss him back. He smelled of wood smoke and soap, and he tasted like whisky. And when she moved her tongue against his, he tensed and his hands went hard against her body, his thumb massaging circles deep into the flesh of her shoulder. His other hand tightened on the soft flesh of her hip to hold her tight to him. She could feel his smile, tingling against her lips.

And then, as quickly the kiss had begun, it was

over. He set her back on her feet again and for a moment they leaned against each other, as though neither were steady enough to stand without support of the other. When he pulled away from her, he shook his head and sighed in satisfaction. He was breathless, as he said, 'That is quite the richest reward I've taken in ages. So much more valuable than mere jewels. I will live on the memory of it for a very long time.' He traced the outline of her lips with the tip of his finger. 'I am sorry for frightening you and I thank you for not crying out. Know that your secrets are as safe with me as mine are with you. And now, if you will excuse me?' He bowed. 'Do not light the candle just yet. Count ten and I will be gone.'

And he turned from her and went to the window, stepping over the sill and out into the darkness.

She rushed to the window after him, and looked out to see him climb down the side of the house and slip across the garden as noiselessly as a shadow, before scaling the stone wall that surrounded it.

He paused as he reached the top and turned back to look towards her. Could he see her there, watching him go, or did he merely suspect?

But she could see him, silhouetted on the top of the garden wall. He was neither dark nor fair. Brown hair, she thought, although it was hard to tell in the moonlight, and dark clothes. A nice build, but she'd felt that when he'd held her. Not a person she recognised.

He blew a kiss in the direction of her open window, swung his legs over the side and dropped from view.

She hurried back into the room and fumbled with a lucifer and a taper, trying to still the beating of her heart. She might not know him, but he knew her. He knew the house and had called her by her title.

And now he knew her secret: she was helpless and alone and nearing the end of her resources. She found this not nearly as threatening as if Lord Barton had known the depth of her poverty. If he had, he'd have used that to his advantage against her.

But the thief had apologised, and taken his leave. And the kiss, of course. But he'd left everything of value, so it was a fair trade. She knelt to pick up the contents of the spilled jewel box, and her foot brushed a black velvet bag on the floor at the side of the dresser.

He must have brought it, meaning to hold the things he took. And it was not empty. As she picked it up, she felt the weight of it shift in her hands.

Dear God, what was she to do now? She could not very well call the man back. He was no longer in the street and she did not know his address.

She did not want to know his address, she reminded herself. He was a criminal. She would look more than forward to seek him out, after the way she had responded to the kiss. And the contents were not his, anyway, so why should they be returned? If the bag contained jewellery, perhaps she could put an ad in *The*

Times, describing the pieces. The rightful owners would step forward, and she might never have to explain how she got them.

She poured the contents of the bag out into her hand. Gold. Guineas filled her hand, and spilled on to the floor.

She tried to imagine the ad she must post, to account for that. 'Will the person who lost a large sum of money on my bedroom floor please identify it…?'

It was madness. There was no way she could return it.

She gathered the money into stacks, counting as she went. This was enough to pay the servants what she owed them, and settle the grocer's bill and next month's expenses as well.

If she kept her tongue and kept the money, she could hold off the inevitable for another month.

But what if the thief came back and demanded to know what had become of his money? She shivered. Then she must hope that he was as understanding as he had been this evening. It would not be so terrible if she must part with another kiss.

Tony arrived at his townhouse in fine spirits, ignored the door before him and smiled at the façade. He rubbed his palms together once, and took a running start at it, jumping to catch the first handhold above the window of the front room. He climbed the next flight easily, his fingers and toes fitting into the familiar places worn into the bricks, then leaned to grasp the edge of the balcony, chinning himself, swinging a leg up and rolling his body lightly over the railing to land on his feet in front of the open doors to his bedroom. He parted the curtains and stepped through. 'Good evening, Patrick.'

His valet had responded with an oath and seized the fireplace poker to defend himself, before recognising his master and trying to turn his movement into an innocuous attempt to adjust the logs in the grate. 'Sir. I believe we have discussed this before. It is a very bad habit, and you have promised to use the front door in the future, just as I have promised to leave it unlocked on nights when you are working.'

Tony grinned back at him. 'I am sorry. I could not help myself. I am—'

Deliriously happy.

'—full of the devil, after this evening's outing. You will never guess who Stanton sent me out to spy on.'

Patrick said nothing, waiting expectantly.

'The Dowager Duchess of Wellford.'

This was worthy of another oath from Patrick. 'And you informed him that you could not.'

'I did no such thing. He was under the impression that she was consorting with Lord John Barton, that they were in league in some sort of nefarious doings involving stolen printing plates. If he had not sent me, it would be someone else. I went post-haste to her rooms for a search. The climb to her bedroom window was—'

As easy as I've always dreamed it to be...

'—no problem. Thank the Lord, there was no sign of anything illegal hidden in her rooms. Although there is evidence that she is in dire straits and in a position to be forced to do things against her nature, by Barton or someone else. And then—and here is the best part, Patrick—while I was searching, she caught me at it.'

'Sir.' Patrick's tone implied that the word 'caught' was not under any circumstances the best part of a story.

'She caught me,' Tony repeated. 'And so I was forced to hold her tight, and question her. And because I wished to be every bit the rogue I appeared to be, I kissed her.'

'And then?' Patrick leaned forward with a certain amount of interest.

Tony sighed. 'And then she kissed me back.'

'And then?' Patrick prompted again.

'And then I climbed out the window and came home. But not before leaving her the purse that Stanton had given me to cover the night's work. I dare say she will not be required to sell the last of her jewellery for quite some time. St John was most generous. It was quite the most perfect evening I've ever had. What say you to that?'

Patrick dropped any attempt at servitude. 'I say, some day, when you are old enough to be shaved, you will be quite a man with the ladies. Ah, but wait. You are thirty, are you not? Then it is quite another matter.'

'And what would you have had me do?'

Patrick was working very hard not to make any of the more obvious suggestions, which might get him sacked. 'You might, at least, have told her the truth.'

'Just what part of it?'

'That you have been pining for her like a moon calf, low these long years.'

'I did tell her. Well, not the truth, as such. Not that truth, at any rate. I told her that she needn't be afraid, which is true. And that I was a most unexceptional fellow. And that I have loved one woman my entire life.' Tony frowned. 'I did not tell her it was her, as such. You might think a woman would be glad to hear that? But trust me, Patrick, when she is hearing it from a stranger who is hiding in her bedroom, it will not be well received.'

'But you are not a stranger to her.'

'But she does not know that. I did not have time to explain the full story. An abbreviated version of the truth, one which omitted my identity, was definitely the order of the day. And despite what you may think of my romantic abilities, I've told the story before and found that omitting the identity of my beloved works in my favour. Nothing softens the heart of a woman quite so much as the story of my hopeless love for another. And how can I resist when they wish to comfort me in my misery?'

'Sir,' said Patrick, in a way that always seemed to mean 'idiot'. 'If you are with the object of the hopeless passion, and you wish the passion to cease being a hopeless one, then the unvarnished truth is usually the best course.'

No longer hopeless...

Tony shook his head. A single kiss was a long way from the fulfilment of his life's romantic fantasies, and it would be foolish to set his heart upon it. 'Nothing will come from this night's meeting. Even if the whole truth is revealed. Think sensibly for a moment, Patrick. Much time has passed since I knew her. She barely knew me then. I doubt she even remembers me. She is a duchess, even if she is a dowager. And while I am her most humble servant, I am most decidedly not, nor ever will be, a duke. Or, for that matter, a marquis, an earl or even a baron. With me, she could live quite comfortably to a ripe old age.' He dismissed his own dreams on that subject with a wave of his hand.

'But should she attach herself to me, it would mean that many doors, which were once opened, would be closed to her. She would go from her Grace the Duchess to plain old Mrs Smythe. In the face of that, an offer of undying devotion is no equal. And the whole town knows her as the most beautiful woman in London. She will not want for suitors, and need not settle for the likes of me. She will aim higher, when she seeks another husband. Man is not meant to have all that he dreams possible. Not in this life, at any rate.'

Patrick applauded with mock-courtesy. 'Most humble, sir. I had forgotten that you studied for the ministry. You have done a most effective job of talking yourself out of the attempt. In winning the hand of a lady, it would be better if you had studied the Romans. *Carpe diem*, sir.'

'I *carpe*-d the situation to the best of my ability, thank you very much.' Tony closed his eyes and remembered the kiss. 'And perhaps there will be other opportunities. I must see her again, in any case, to settle the business with Barton and to make sure she is all right.'

He remembered the missing ornaments and the empty jewel box. 'Stanton is wrong. I am sure of it. He told me she was Barton's mistress. But if Barton is keeping her, he is doing it on the cheap. If she were mine, her jewel box would be full to overflowing.'

If she were mine...

'But it is almost empty. And there is evidence that she is selling off the furnishings of the house to make ends meet. I had assumed that that old ninny Wellford would make provision for her after his death. Surely he did not think taking a young wife would somehow extend his own time on this mortal coil. He must have known she'd outlive him.'

He sat in his favourite armchair and stared into the

fire. 'She is putting up a brave front, Patrick, but things are not right, above stairs. The least I can do, as an old friend of the family, is see to it that she comes through this safely.'

Patrick snorted, and poured him his brandy. 'What utter nonsense. Yes, that is the least you could do. And I do not see why you feel it necessary to pretend that you wish to do as little as possible. It astounds me that someone who has no trouble taking things which do not belong to him balks when there is a chance to take the thing he most wants.'

Tony took the proffered glass and gestured with it. 'She is not some inanimate object, Patrick. I cannot just go and take her. She has a say in the matter.'

Patrick shook his head, giving his master up as hopeless, and, totally forgetting his station, poured a brandy for himself. 'Not the woman, sir. Happiness. You are so accustomed to thinking in terms of what you might do for others that you forget to do what might be in your own best interests. By all means, empty your purse and risk your fool neck helping the woman, if it pleases you to do so.

'But when the moment comes to collect a reward for it, do not stand upon your honour and deny yourself what pleasure you can gain from the moment. Do not think twice about your inability to rival her late husband in rank or pocketbook. If, in the end, the woman cares only for those, you must admit you have been wrong about her, and the girl you loved no longer exists. No matter how beautiful she may be, if she is a fortune hunter, then she is not worth saving and you are best off to forget her.'

Chapter Four

Constance sat in her morning room, paging through the small stack of receipts in front of her. It was ever so much more satisfying than the stack of overdue bills that had been there just a few days before. She was a long way from safe. But neither was she standing on the edge of financial disaster, staring down into total ruin.

She would need to visit the new duke, to remind him of his promised allowance, which would cover the incoming bills. And while there, she could retrieve the deed. With that in hand, she might secure a loan against the house, or arrange its sale. With money of her own in her pocket, she might protect herself against the vagaries of Freddy's payments for many months to come. For the first time in ages, she felt the stirrings of hope for the future, and cautious optimism.

And her salvation had come from a strange source,

indeed. She offered a silent prayer of thanks for the timely intervention of the thief, whoever he might be, and hoped that the loss of his little bag had not forced him to do other crimes. She would hate to think herself the cause of misfortune in others, or the further ruination of the man that had climbed out of her window.

But, somehow, she suspected it was not the case. Perhaps she was romanticising a criminal, and most foolish for it. She might be creating a Robin Hood out of a common scoundrel. But the situation had been so fortuitous, it almost seemed that hc had meant to leave the money behind for her use.

It was a ludicrous notion. What reason would he have had to help her? But he had offered, had he not? And if he had not meant to leave it, he must have missed the bag by now. Surely he would have returned to take it from her? After she was sure he was gone, she had gathered the money back into the sack, and placed it under her pillow. And then she had lain awake in dread most of the night, convinced that at any moment, she would feel a breeze at the window and hear a light step on the carpet, approaching her bed in the darkness…

And at last she had forced herself to admit that it was not dread she was feeling at the reappearance of the strange man. The idea that he would return and she might open her eyes to find him bending over her bed and reaching to touch her, held no terror, just a rush of passionate emotion fuelled by the memory of a stolen kiss.

Which was utterly ridiculous. It had been a very nice kiss. And best to leave it at that. He was a thief, and she would be a fool to trust him with her heart or her reputation, despite what he had said to her the previous night.

And even if he were a gentleman, as he claimed, what could they possibly have in common other than a single moment of weakness? Could she have a conversation with him, in the light of day? Would he even wish to see her? He had said something about being in love. Did he care for her at all? Kisses meant very little to most men. He had probably forgotten it already.

But it had been a most extraordinary kiss.

Her mind had circled back again, to replay the kiss, as it seemed to do whenever she tried to talk herself out of the fantasy. She was fast creating a paragon out of nothing. A man both dashing and kind, but more than a bit of a rogue. When the candles were lit, he would be passably good-looking, and as innocuous in appearance and behaviour as he had claimed. But at night, he was a burglar, living off his wits. And a single kiss from her would make him forsake all others and risk capture by returning to her rooms.

She closed her eyes and smiled, imagining his arms about her again. He would confess that he was unable to resist the attraction, and assure her that, if she could find it in her heart to forgive his criminal misdeeds, he would love and cherish her 'til the end of her days.

'Your Grace, there is a gentleman here to see you.'

Susan was standing in the door, hesitating to interrupt. And for a moment, Constance thought that her dream had come to life. She looked enquiringly to her maid.

'Lord Barton.'

Damn.

'Tell him I am not at home, Susan.'

'He is most insistent, your Grace.'

'As am I. I am not now, nor ever shall be, at home to Lord Barton.'

'I thought you might say that.' The voice came from the hall, just beyond Susan's head. 'So I took the liberty of letting myself in. I hope you don't mind.' Jack Barton's tone made it clear that he didn't care one way or the other whether she minded—he intended to do as he pleased in the matter.

Constance swept the papers she'd been holding under the desk blotter to hide them, and stood to face him.

'I mind very much, Lord Barton.'

'I believe I requested, when last we talked, that you call me Jack.' He was smiling, as though he had totally forgotten her response to their last conversation.

'And then you insulted me.'

'I meant the offer as a compliment, your Grace. I do not make it lightly, nor do I make such generous offers to all the women of my acquaintance.'

'You suggested that I become your mistress,' she reminded him, coldly.

'Because I wish to surround myself with beauty, and can afford to do so. You are quite the most beautiful woman I have ever seen, and I mean to have you.'

'I am not some item, to be added to your collection,' she replied. 'You are mistaken, if you think you can purchase a woman as easily as a painting.'

He was unaffected by her answer. 'I have not been so in the past. For the most part, it is only a matter of finding the correct price. Once you do, you can purchase anything.'

'Let me make myself clear: you cannot buy me, Lord Barton. No amount of money would induce me to submit to you. Now, get out of my house.' She pointed towards the door.

'No.'

This presented a problem. She could not put him out herself, and such male servants as she had were either too young or too old to do the job for her. To a gentleman, her demand that he leave should have been enough. But if she was forced to rely on Barton's honour as a gentleman, she was left with nothing at all to defend herself. 'Very well, then,' she said, resigned. 'State your business and then be gone.'

He smiled and took a seat in the chair near her desk, as though he were a welcome guest. 'I expected you would see it my way, once you had thought about it. I came about the ball I am hosting, tomorrow evening.'

'I sent regrets.'

'Yes, you did. You are the picture of courtesy, if a trifle stubborn. I must break you of that, if we are to manage well together.'

'Do not think you need to manage me, Lord Barton,' she snapped back at him. 'I thought I made it clear, when I refused your contemptible offer, that we would not be doing anything further together. I do not wish to dance with you. I doubt I can eat in your presence, since the thought of you sickens me. And thus, I sent regrets for your ball.'

Her word seemed to have no effect on his continued good humour. He was still smiling as he said, 'That is not acceptable.'

'It is most acceptable to me,' she insisted. 'And that is all that matters. I doubt that you have any tender feelings that I might have offended. I do not believe you capable of them.'

'Let me speak plainly,' he said.

'I have been unable to stop you.'

'You will be in attendance at the ball, because I wish it to be so.'

'And why would I care what you wish?'

Without another word, he reached into his pocket, and withdrew an object, wrapped in a linen handkerchief. His eyes widened and his mouth made an 'Oh', like a conjuror performing a trick. Then he dipped his fingers into the bundle and withdrew a ruby-and-diamond necklace. He dangled it in front of her.

And without thinking, she reached for it, and cursed her hand for acting faster than her wits.

'I knew you would not be bribed with pretty words or baubles like a sensible woman, since I've tried that and failed. But then I thought, perhaps I was using the wrong bait.'

She watched the necklace, glittering in his hand, and tried to conceal her desire for it.

'You were most foolish to sell the whole thing. You needn't have made a complete copy you know. Just pried out the stones and let the jeweller fit paste ones into the old setting.'

She had learned that herself, after selling the rubies. The cost of even the cheapest copy ate almost all of the additional profit from selling the gold setting.

She said nothing.

He turned the necklace to let the jewels sparkle in the sunlight. 'And you made the copy, once you realised that the necklace was not technically yours, did you not? It is part of your husband's entail. It belongs to the new duke, and not to you. It was very wrong of you to sell it. What do you suppose the new duke would say, if he knew you were selling a necklace that has been in his family for generations?'

The new duke would likely go many months before noticing its absence. When he did, she'd hoped to stall him with the copy until she could afford to buy back the real necklace. But she kept her foolish mouth shut over the secret since Barton had enough power over her without her full confession.

'I trust you have seen the error of your ways, and do not wish to continue stealing from your nephew.'

She thought to argue that it was not really stealing, if one was only trying to get money that one was owed, and continued to hold silent.

He nodded as though she had spoken. 'Fortunately for you, I am an understanding man. I will give you back your necklace. Once you have done something for me.'

She closed her eyes. Now she must decide. Lie with Barton, or let him go to Freddy with the necklace. The choice was easy. Let him tell Freddy the truth. Perhaps it would move the duke to loosen his purse strings.

When she opened her eyes again, Barton was watching her with amusement. 'You are not asking what it is I wish.'

'I know what it is that you want. The answer is still no.'

He laughed. 'You think I demand unconditional surrender, for a single strand of rubies? While it is a lovely necklace, I suspect you hold your honour to be worth more. A price above rubies, perhaps?' He laughed. 'Listen carefully to my offer, and then give me your answer.

'First, what will happen to you, if you deny me: I will let the necklace fall from my pocket somewhere public. Everyone knows it is yours. Someone will ask me how I came by it. I will explain how you left it in my rooms. The world will draw its own conclusions, and you will be ruined.

'Or you can attend the ball tomorrow. You will stand beside me as hostess, and dance with me as I wish. At the end of the evening, I will return the jewels to you, and you may go home.'

'And if I stand up with you, the world will draw much the same conclusions that they did, if I do not obey you,' she said.

'They might wonder, but they will not be sure.'

She weighed the possibilities. The ruby necklace was clear proof of her perfidy. If she could retrieve it without much cost to her honour, it would be worth the attempt. Of course, there was a chance that he would deny her.

He saw the suspicion in her eyes. 'You needn't fear. I swear that you shall have the thing back before the clock strikes twelve. And I do not expect physical intimacy. Not yet, at any rate. But if you think you can toy with me, or trick me in some way, the price for the necklace may be much higher the next time I offer it.'

What was she to do? It was not really such a great sacrifice to go to a ball. Although she hated Barton, it would do her reputation no real harm. 'Very well. I will attend.'

He laughed, again. It was a cold sound, short and

brittle like cracking ice. 'Excellent. I shall have the pleasure of your company, and you shall have your necklace.'

He leaned closer, the laughter gone from his voice. 'And you will have learned a valuable lesson. When things go my way, I am happy and reward those around me. Rewards are so much better than punishment, are they not? I find that training a woman is not much different than training a hound. It all begins with the smallest act of obedience. Once a man has achieved that, he is well on the road to becoming a master.' There was a half-smile of satisfaction on his face, as though his eventual victory was a foregone conclusion.

'You will find, Lord Barton, that I am not some lap-dog to be easily brought to heel. You have won in this. But that is all. Now, if you will excuse me, I must prepare for your ball tomorrow. I wish to look my best, so that you may remember me well, for it will be the last time that you see me. If you please.' She gestured to the door.

He rose, indolently, and proceeded out of the room, leaving the air around her bitterly cold.

Constance waited in the drawing room of the London townhouse of the current Duke of Wellford. She had no right to feel the wave of possessiveness that she was feeling towards the house and its contents.

It did not belong to her, after all. It had been her husband's home long before she married him, but never truly hers. She had seen to the care and cleaning of it, of course. She had entertained guests in this very room. She had chosen the furnishings, and the food. She had hired and fired the servants.

And now, after twelve years in residence, and only a year away, she was a visitor. The butler who had greeted her was not familiar. When crossing the entrance hall, she caught sight of a footman she had hired herself. He had almost smiled when he'd seen her. Almost. And then there had been a flash of pity, before he went back to his duties, and treated her with the excessive formality due a ranking guest, and not a member of the family.

And to add to the discomfort, Freddy left her to wait. She had informed him that morning that she'd planned to visit, but when she arrived he was not in attendance, having decided to go riding in Hyde Park with his friends.

Robert had often railed against the folly of keeping horses in town. To keep the beasts fed, groomed and stabled was disproportionately expensive, when compared to the amount of time he had to ride while residing in the city. Apparently, the new duke had no such concerns.

Constance drummed her fingers against the small gilt table beside the settee, then folded her hands in her lap, willing them to be still. It was best to marshal her patience before Freddy arrived, if she wished to greet him pleasantly and keep him in good humour. She would make no ground in securing money or deed if she angered him by censuring his behaviour.

Especially if she must admit to him that she'd pawned the family jewels to pay the butcher's bill. He would see such behaviour as a weakness in her own character, and not his own for denying her funds and leaving her in need. She had learned from past discussions that, although Freddy was nearly useless at his best, if she angered him or questioned his judgement he could be even worse.

She had refused a servant's offer of refreshment for the third time before Freddy deigned to grace her with his presence, still in his riding coat. The smell of horses followed him into the room, and she noticed, with distaste, that there was mud from the stable still on his boot. He was tracking it on the Aubusson.

Not her Aubusson, she reminded herself. And not her problem. Someone would clean it. It did not matter.

'Aunt Constance, to what do I owe the pleasure?' There was a moment's awkwardness as he greeted her, and remembered that he was her better, and not a guest in her house.

'I wish it were only for pleasure that I am visiting, your Grace.' She rose to greet him, dropping a respectful curtsy.

'Please, Constance. Call me Freddy.' There was still

the touch of a little boy's pleading as he said it. 'You can, you know. I want you to treat this as though it were your home. It can be your home in truth, if you wish. Lord knows, I could use a woman with a level head to run the household for me.'

And how could she tell him that she could not bear to? The memories of Robert were still fresh in her mind. The knowledge that the servants were no longer hers to command, and that she could, and should be, displaced when Freddy took a wife of his own—she tried not to shudder at the thought.

'You know I must not, Freddy. It is no longer my place. It would be far better were you to find a wife to take the house in hand.'

He scoffed. 'Settle down so soon? Surely there is time for that later. I am just learning to enjoy the advantages of the title. A wife would spoil it all.'

She dreaded to think what advantages he had discovered that would be so hindered by a wife. 'It is your duty, you know,' she reminded, as gently as possible.

Freddy shook his head like a stubborn child. 'All you ever talk of is duty, Aunt Constance. There is more to life than doing one's duty.'

'Duty is much a part of your position, Freddy. You have a responsibility to your King, to your tenants, to your servants.' She hoped that the responsibility to herself was implied, and that he would not make her beg for her allowance.

'Well, yes. I suppose. But Parliament is not currently in session. So there is one thing I needn't worry about. And the tenants take care of themselves, for the most part.'

She resisted the urge to point out that they never seemed to manage it, when her husband was alive. 'But there is still the matter of the collecting of rents, and the paying of bills, and making sure that all your financial obligations are met.' And there was a broad enough hint, if he cared to take it.

'But it is a tiresome business to worry over every little detail, when the sun is shining and one is aching for a gallop.' Although Freddy's dirty boots had come home, his mind was still on horseback in the park.

'An estate manager, or man of business, can take care of such things. It would leave you with less to worry about.'

'But, Aunt Constance, I am not worried now.' As Freddy smiled, it was evident that her financial problems had in no way touched him. 'And being duke is not so hard as all that, I'm sure. With a little practice, I can manage the estates on my own, just as Uncle Robert did.'

Constance fought the urge to inform Freddy how distant his abilities were from those of his uncle. She took a deep breath, and tried a different way. 'I am sure you are right, Freddy. Once you have held the title for a while, you will have everything set to rights.

But I must admit, right now, that I was rather hoping we could deal with the part of the estate that concerns my allowance. It worries me greatly, that I have not received this month's cheque, and in the past, the amount—' she took another breath and rushed through the next words '—has not been sufficient to cover expenses.'

'You know,' said Freddy, as though the thought had just occurred to him, 'that if you were to live in the dower house of the manor, your expenses would not be so very great.'

'They are not great now, I assure you. I have made what economies I can.' A year of mutton instead of lamb, and no shopping, and cuts in staff had done nothing to make the income match the outflow.

'But really, Aunt Constance. Be sensible. If you were to leave London and return to the country, I need not give you any allowance at all.' He was smiling as though he had found the perfect solution.

'That is not technically true, Freddy,' she said. 'I still must eat. And pay my maid. And there are dresses to buy, carriages to hire, small entertainments… The only way you will be free of the expense of me is when I re-marry and my upkeep falls upon my husband.'

He stared at her as though the idea had never oc-curred to him. 'Surely you do not mean to remarry so soon, Aunt Constance.'

'On the contrary, Freddy, I find it a most respectable

choice. I am sure that Robert would have had no problem with it. He said as much to me, when he was alive. And he always meant me to set up housekeeping in town, in hopes that I might meet someone suitable, and not be too much alone. For that reason, he deeded me the house in Grosvenor Square. Speaking of which...' she eased the conversation towards her next request '...if possible, I would like to take the deed away with me today, to give to my bankers.'

Freddy's brow furrowed. 'I never saw the logic in Uncle Robert's deeding the house to you, Aunt Constance. It is too much responsibility for a woman, in my opinion. As I told you before, you are welcome here, or in the dower house, in Sussex. It is very nice.'

She had to hide her annoyance before continuing. 'I have no doubt it is a nice house, Freddy. I decorated it myself, for Robert's mother. And I have no problem staying in it. When I visit,' she said, slowly and clearly. 'But I have no wish to move back to Sussex. Robert meant for me to be out in London, after he died, mixing freely with society.'

'But why must it be London? Society in the country was quite good enough for you before.'

'Although the country life is most pleasant, I know the gentlemen in the neighbourhood, and can assure you there is no one to suit me, in regards to matrimony. I am not likely to meet a husband if I cloister myself in the dower house.'

'If you are there, where I can keep an eye on you, I can advise you, if and when it comes to the matter of your marriage.'

If and when she married? 'Freddy,' she said, struggling to maintain her temper, 'I am not a child that needs advice in this matter. I am a full six years older than you, and will know a good match when I see it. I do not need your advice, or your permission.'

'But you do need my money,' he pointed out, petulantly.

'Not for so very much longer, I hope. I am endeavouring to be out of your hair and your pocketbook with as much expedience as I can manage. But you need to help me in this, Freddy.' She softened. 'Please. If you will give me my allowance, I can pay my bills and will not bother you again for quite some time. Perhaps never. If you give me the deed, I can dispense with the house, and move to simpler accommodations. It will mean less expense for both of us.'

Freddy looked uncomfortable. 'The deed is fine where it is. I really do not see the need to bother you with the care of it.'

'Oh, it is no bother, Freddy,' she assured him. 'It makes sense, does it not, to keep it with the rest of my papers? And it will be one less thing you need to keep track of.'

His eyes darted around the room, as though looking for some excuse to escape the conversation. 'I mean…really, Constance, you cannot expect me to lay hands on the thing, on such short notice.'

'Freddy, it is not short notice at all. I have asked you for it for the better part of a year. Please can you not go into the study and bring it to me? Then I will be gone and you need not hear me ask again.'

'Well, the truth is, Constance…' Freddy looked more than uncomfortable, now, and had to struggle to meet her gaze '…the truth is, I have lost it.'

'Do not be ridiculous, Freddy. I know it lies in the safe, in my husband's—I mean, in your study. You could get it for me now, if you wished.'

'Constance, you do not understand.'

'Clearly I don't, Freddy. Let us go to the study, now. I will show you where it is.'

His voice was lower, almost hard to hear, and he was looking at the ground. 'It is no longer in the safe, Constance. As I told you, I lost it.'

'Well, then let us go and search for it. It is probably among the papers in your desk.' She could not resist a reproof. 'Although it might have been wiser to never have removed it from the safe. It would have saved the bother now.'

'At cards, Constance.' He said it loud and looked her straight in the eye. 'It is not on the desk, or anywhere else in the house. I lost it at cards. I was in my cups, and in deep play. And I am a little short of cash, until the next rents are collected.'

'And so you paid your debt with a thing that does not belong to you.' She looked at him in horror, as she realised just how bad things had become.

She no longer bothered to contain her temper. 'I come here at my wits' end, without a penny in my pocket, and you berate me for the high price of my keeping. You tell me I only want your money. As I see it, Freddy, I do not need your money nearly so much as you needed mine. You took the only thing I had that truly belonged to me and you gambled it away. And you did it because you are too busy drinking and gaming and whoring to be bothered to collect the rents on your properties, which you need to do to keep the coffers full. And now you think you can force me back to the country to play housekeeper to you, while you destroy everything my husband worked so hard to build.'

'I am the duke now,' he shouted back, although he sounded more like a spoiled child than a peer of the realm. 'Not your husband. I do not have to take advice or listen to you criticise my methods. I can do as I please.'

'Then you do not understand what it means to be a duke. Not a good one, at any rate,' she snapped.

'Good or bad, Aunt Constance, it would serve you to do as I say, for I am head of your family now. Uncle Robert was a fool to give you as much freedom as he did, for you seem to think that you can do just as you please, and answer to no one. I am glad that the deed is gone, and I no longer need hear you whine for it. It is time that this stupidity of maintaining an expensive residence in London is brought to a halt, and you are brought to your senses.

'And with regard to your allowance—you will have no more money from me, not another groat, until you come to your senses and move to the dower house at Wellford, where you belong.'

Chapter Five

At the door of the ballroom in Barton's home, Constance greeted her guests with a frozen smile. If she could manage to control nothing else around her, she could at least control her temper for the few hours necessary to earn back her necklace.

She had pleaded with Freddy to see reason, and he had all but thrown her from his house. He would not even tell her who held the deed to her own home, and she was left to wait for a knock at the door, politely explaining that she must pay rent or vacate the premises.

And tonight she must dance to Barton's tune, if only to retrieve the necklace and sell the stones again. The rubies would mean another month's income, perhaps two. Or even more if she was forced to reduce her staff and move to a smaller place.

But it did no good to think about what might come,

if there was a more immediate problem to deal with. Until she had the rubies in hand, she must keep a tight rein on her emotions, and give Barton what he wanted. To that end, she made sure that she looked her best, and was ready when the carriage he'd sent for her arrived. Her gown was not new, but she had not worn it in over a year. Susan had retrimmed the deep blue satin with silver lace, and dressed her dark hair with silver ribbons.

Constance was afraid to wear the necklace that best suited the gown lest someone recognise the sapphires as paste, and settled for the pearls. And she made sure that there was enough empty space in her reticule to carry away the rubies, should Barton be true to his word and return them to her.

Of course, if he did not, she would feel most foolish for being rooked into attending the evening's affair. But it would be a small loss, and the trick would not work twice. If she did not have the rubies at the end of the evening, she would reconcile herself to whatever might result from Barton's revelation.

But at the moment she was trapped in the receiving line next to a man she detested, and forced to entertain his guests as if they were her own. She smiled politely at the man bent over her hand, smiled at his wife as well, and responded to their greetings by rote, as she had to hundreds of guests at parties she had thrown for Robert. Her smile brightened as she noticed them to be strangers. Barton was not privy to the first circle of

the *ton*. Many of her closest friends recognised the man
for what he was and declined the invitation, or cut him
outright. Constance wholeheartedly regretted that she
had been slow to see his true character, but she was not
alone, for the ballroom was full of people willing to
befriend him.

She looked past the next man in line, barely hearing Barton's introduction of him, and scanned the
crowd. Of course, a fair portion of the guests were social climbers, cits and hangers-on. But after this evening, she need never see them again, and they certainly
would not be in a position to go gossiping to her friends
about seeing her here.

'Mr Smythe, the Dowager Duchess of Wellford.'
She winced. Barton insisted on using her title to his
friends, as though he wished to make sure that everyone knew the value of his new possession.

The man before her bowed low over her hand. 'Your
Grace.'

Although his face was unfamiliar, his voice struck
a chord of memory. There was laughter in it. And the
touch of his hand on hers was at the same time, ordinary and intimately familiar.

It was the thief from her bedroom.

He rose from his bow and looked into her eyes for
a fraction of a second too long, as though daring her
to speak and knowing she could not. His eyes were
hazel and sparkling from the shared conspiracy, his

smile was broad and a trifle too intense for a common introduction. If it were another man, she might think he had arrived half-foxed and up to mischief. But this man had already proven to be more than he appeared. If he meant to cause trouble, she doubted he would blame an excess of wine.

'Mr Smythe?' That was what Barton had said, had he not? She could not very well ask him to repeat himself, or demand to know how he knew Smythe. To express too much interest in a male guest was not the quickest way back to her necklace.

Of course, she could wipe the familiar grin from Smythe's face, and prove to him that she recognised him. A casual word could ruin him just as quickly as it could her. She opened her mouth.

And perhaps he would ask about the money she'd stolen from him or the kiss he'd stolen in her bedroom.

She closed her mouth again, and pasted on a delighted smile. 'How do you do, Mr Smythe.'

'Quite well, thank you.' She could swear he winked at her.

And then, he was gone.

If Barton had noticed anything pass between them, he said nothing. And soon the guests were through the line and Barton led her out in the first dance of the evening.

She moved through the patterns as if sleepwalking, speaking to her partner only when she could not avoid it. He danced with her several more times, when she could not manage to dodge his attention, and she maintained the same demeanour: polite, cordial and distant. Nothing that might make the guests assume there was anything of a more intimate nature likely to happen between them in the future.

And while she held Barton at a distance, she also managed to avoid contact with the curious Mr Smythe. It was possible that she had imagined recognising him. Perhaps she had been wrong. She could not very well ask him about it in a crowded ballroom.

But she was sure she was not mistaken. He was the thief. She had seen the recognition in his eyes. And she was somewhat frustrated to realise that it was not to be the least like she had fantasised, with him carrying some burning desire to see her again. She thought she could feel him, observing her from across the room, but this might be her imagination as well. He made no attempt to contact her; when she looked in his direction, he was always looking elsewhere. He seemed to care very little that she was in the room at all.

She was relieved when it finally came time for supper. Barton led her into the dining room, and her position as hostess meant that she was seated at the far end of the table from him. But nowhere near Smythe, either. The people around her were unexceptional, and she relaxed for a time, chatting amiably with them before the meal ended and she had to gather her wits and return to the dance floor.

When she reached the ballroom, she took care to get lost in the crowd and separated from her host. The next dance was a waltz, far more intimate than she liked, if she should have to dance with Barton. If she could find another partner quickly, it would be several minutes before she need speak with him again. She searched the room. Quickly, someone. Anyone.

'Your Grace, may I have this dance?'

She'd said yes to the man before even turning to face him. And when she looked up, it was into the smiling eyes of Mr Smythe.

He saw her discomposure and said nothing, taking her hand and leading her out on to the floor.

As the music began, any doubt that he was the man from her bedroom disappeared. He held her as he had held her that night, in a grasp that managed to be both relaxed and intimate. It felt good to be in his arms again, and to be able to admire him in the candlelight.

And there was much about him that was admirable. His hair was brown, and had an appealing softness to it. She remembered how it had felt when she'd touched it, and wanted to touch it again. He had pleasant, even features, and the smile on his lips gave every indication of breaking into a grin, given the slightest provocation. His eyes were bright with suppressed mirth. If his profession left him racked with guilt, there was no indication of it, for he seemed a most happy fellow.

They danced in silence, until at last he leaned a trifle closer and whispered, 'How long do you suppose we can pretend a lack of recognition to each other? We have managed quite well so far, I think. Longer than I expected. But one of us has to break eventually. I surrender. You have won.'

'I don't know what you are talking about.'

'And now you are taking the game to extra innings. Not necessary. I am conquered. Vanquished. You nearly had me in the receiving line, you know. Finding you there, next to Barton, was a nasty surprise.'

'You will survive it,' she responded tartly. 'Seeing an acquaintance unexpectedly in a public place is not nearly so shocking as finding a total stranger in one's private rooms.'

'*Touché*. But I had hoped you had forgiven me for that. Why so cold to me now?'

'Perhaps I don't approve of people who take things that don't belong to them.'

'Oh, really? But I notice, when you were in need, that you had no problem keeping the money I left for you.'

So he had left it for her. But did he expect thanks for involving her in a theft? 'That was different. What else was I to do with it? I had no idea—'

'Where to find me and who the money belonged to. And you were in desperate need, so you took it. Believe me, I understand completely.'

'I will pay you back when I am able,' she said.

'You will pay me back tonight,' he replied.

Her heart sank. He had seemed so nice. And he had promised not to compromise her. Now he would become just another man with a hold over her, and he would use it to his advantage like all the rest. She stumbled as they turned.

He caught her, incorporating the misstep gracefully into the movement of the dance. 'Oh, do not give me that melodramatic look. We are in a ballroom, not Drury Lane. I have no intention of asking you to whore yourself to me. I merely need you to keep your lover, Barton, occupied while I go to search his study.'

'He is not my lover,' she retorted.

'Really? But you stand as hostess, at his side.'

'It was not my desire to do so.'

'And you have been seen often in his company.'

'For a time,' she corrected, 'but no more after to-night. He is nothing singular. I have been seen in the company of many men.'

His eyebrow arched suggestively.

'I am in your company now. But that does not mean I would invite you to my bed.'

Of course, if he wished to be there, he would hardly require an invitation. She would be quite helpless to stop him, and perhaps next time he would wish to steal more than a kiss. Once the thought was formed, it showed no intention of fading.

He was staring at her again, noticing the gap in the conversation. And his smile was definitely a grin. She wished she had not mentioned the bed at all, for if he did not have the idea before, he must surely be thinking of it now.

She cleared her throat. 'What I meant to say was, I hope to marry again, and that means I am likely to be seen in the company of gentleman who I think might be of a mind to take a wife.'

'And you chose Barton as a possible husband?' Smythe's tone was incredulous and the smile disappeared from his face.

'I sometimes find that the interests of gentlemen are less than worthy. It is a tribute to my naïveté and not my lowered standards.'

'So you and Barton are not…?' He spoke a trifle too hastily and his hand tightened on her waist.

'He made an offer that had nothing to do with matrimony, and I gave him a set-down. More than once.' She frowned. 'At the end of the evening I will probably have to give him another, since he ignored the others. And he tricked me into coming here, for reasons I'd rather not discuss.'

He blinked down at her and his hand relaxed. He was holding her in the same loose grip as before, as though he was confident that she would stay with him, even if he had no hold on her. 'Well, then. Perhaps I was misinformed.'

'Most definitely you were.'

He looked bemused. 'Then I hope you will not think

it too rude when I will ask you to keep the man who is not your lover, though he seems to think he will be, occupied while I pay an unaccompanied visit to his study.'

'And how do you expect me to do that?'

'Use your imagination. A quarter of an hour is all I need and easily worth the hundred guineas I left in your room.'

The dance came to an end and he led her from the floor. 'Your Grace, it was an unexpected pleasure. Now, if you will excuse me?' There was the slightest inclination of his head, which seemed to hint that he had business to attend to, and that the clock was ticking.

She glanced across the room, and somewhere in the distance a clock chimed the three-quarter hour. Very well, then. She would give him fifteen minutes. It was a small price for the money he had given her. She glanced around the room, searching for Barton, and saw him too close to the stairs that must lead to the study. 'My lord?' She had hoped to ask him to dance, and out of the corner of her eye, noticed that the orchestra had chosen that inopportune moment to take refreshment. Very well, then. It was near enough the end of the evening. Now was as good a time as any to retrieve the necklace. 'If I might speak to you?'

'Certainly, my dear.' He bowed low over her hand. 'What is it?'

She resisted the urge to inform him that she was not now, nor ever wished to be, his dear. 'In private.'

'My study, then.' He turned to lead her to the exact place that she did not wish to be.

'Not so private as all that, I think. The garden, perhaps? It is quiet enough there.'

'And most romantic in the moonlight.'

She bit back another retort. There would be time enough in fifteen minutes to set him straight.

He took her hand and led her to the balcony doors, and, at the back of her mind, she felt a minute pass. And another, as he led her outside, and down the stone steps to the garden. When they were in the darkness and a distance from the house, he turned to her and smiled. 'To what do I owe this sudden desire to be alone with me? Have you reconsidered my offer?'

'You know very well the reason. Have I performed to your satisfaction in this little farce?'

'Most admirably. We can make it a regular occurrence, if you wish.'

'But I do not wish,' she said firmly. 'I have told you over and over again.'

'And yet, you agreed to do it tonight. And it was a delightful evening. Not so terrible as you made it out to be, I'm sure.'

'There was only one reason I agreed to come, and you know it full well.'

'Ah, the necklace.' He reached into his pocket, and produced the rubies, holding them in front of her.

She snatched the thing from his hand and secreted it in her reticule, turning to go back to the house, no longer caring about Smythe and his fifteen minutes.

Barton's fingers closed on her upper arm, holding her in place. She attempted to pull away, and he tightened his grip, ever so slightly. To struggle further might leave bruises on her skin. She imagined the shame of going back into the ballroom, the red marks of a man's fingers already blossoming on her arm.

She stayed still.

'Willing to stay with me, after all?'

'I do not wish my behaviour to create gossip.'

He smiled, realising that he'd won again. 'And why would a rumour frighten you? If I am in the wrong, and you do not wish to be with me, then surely you could appeal to one of the many gentlemen of your acquaintance for assistance?' He snapped his fingers. 'But that is right. Many of the gentlemen here have received setdowns from you, have they not? They are likely to be more sympathetic to my plight. Over and over again, you allow men to lead you to the fence, and then you do not jump.'

'That is not the way it has been at all,' she argued. 'I had no idea that the gentlemen in question did not intend marriage. Or you, for that matter. I never sought anything less.'

Barton smiled. 'How refreshingly naïve you are. I think it is the combination of experience and naïveté that attracts me to you. You believe it is possible to go back to the way things were, before you married, and to have a second chance at a husband and a family. But you will never again be that young and innocent. When men look at you, they know that you are too old to guarantee a first child, but fully ripe for all the pleasures that a man might wish to experience with a woman. When we look at you, my dear, we know that you know precisely what will happen when you are alone with us.'

He smiled and drew closer. 'I can see it, even now. The lust sizzles in your eyes. You fear scandal, more than you fear my touch. I can steal a kiss, perhaps a caress in the darkness. These things do not alarm you so much as the thought that someone might catch us at it. I suspect that you would have no problem giving yourself freely, if you could be assured of the discretion of your partner. Take this instance. If you do not submit, you must walk away from me, and I have but to call out and draw attention to the fact that you are with me, or squeeze your arm, ever so slightly.' He tightened his grip, and then relaxed it again, as he felt her submit. 'Then people will notice that we were alone together, and there will be even more talk than there already is.'

'People will think you a brute for forcing yourself on a woman.'

'Since the woman is yourself, and you just spent the evening at my side as hostess, I doubt that anyone will assume force. It is far more likely that they will assume you were a willing participant in anything that might have occurred. The assumptions of a curious society will be confirmed, the minute you complain. Or you can allow me to kiss you, here in the dark, and we can return to the ballroom separately. No one will be the wiser.'

Damn her for her foolishness in thinking she could win against Barton in his own house. She had gained the necklace, only to lose more ground. And damn Mr Smythe for using her as well. He had been gone more than fifteen minutes, she was sure of it. And he thought nothing of leaving her in the clutches of Barton. Now that Smythe had what he wanted, he had forgotten her.

It would do no good to fight Barton now. If she gave in, perhaps the incident would pass quickly, and she might escape. She closed her eyes and tipped her head up to meet him as he leaned in and kissed her.

And she did nothing to stop him, because he was right. The last thing she needed was more gossip. When he wished for her to open her mouth, she did that as well. She could but hope that he would not take things too far in so public a place. And after tonight, scandal or no, she would not be alone with him again.

He was doing his best to arouse feelings in her, and she took great pleasure in ignoring the attempt. If he wished to make love to her, then let him. But eventually, when she did not respond, he would lose interest and let her go. In the meantime, she would see to it that the experience was not so pleasurable as he imagined.

He was working industriously on her mouth, and his hands were on her shoulders. It was only a matter of time before they strayed lower.

She was disappointed to find that she felt neither desire nor outrage at the fact. Her mind felt strangely detached from her body, uninterested in the proceedings and wishing only to go home and put the experience behind her. Let him do what he wished and be done with it. It had been so long since she'd felt anything at all, she doubted that Barton could move her with his fumblings.

As though he'd heard her thoughts, Barton's hand began a slow descent towards the swell of her breast.

And then he pulled away from her with an oath. There was the sound of someone crashing clumsily through the ornamental shrubbery, soft, tuneless whistling growing louder as the intruder approached.

Barton took off in the direction of the sound. 'Here, you. What do you think you're doing?'

'Trying to find my way out of this damn briar patch.'

Constance strangled a laugh. It was Mr Smythe, making it clear to all within earshot that he was done with whatever business he'd been up to.

'I only wanted a breath of air. Two steps from the house and I was lost in the wilderness. I've a good mind to complain to the host.'

'I am the host, you drunken idiot. And you're stepping on my rose-bushes.' Jack was furious.

Constance stepped off the path and disappeared into the darkness, leaning against a tree and giving way to silent giggles.

There was a pause as an apparently drunken Smythe took stock of the situation. 'Roses? So I am. Oh, well. No harm done. The spindly little things were half-dead, anyway. Could have used more water.'

'They are in perfect health. And they are imported from France.'

'Well, that's your problem. Get yourself some proper English flowers. Just as pretty and not so delicate.'

'Get off of my yard, you drunken buffoon! I invited you here, Smythe, on the recommendation of a friend. I can see I was mistaken in the courtesy and it will not be repeated. Kindly take yourself from the premises, before I have you forcibly removed.'

'I was going. Going. Know where I'm not wanted.' She could hear more crashing, as Smythe wandered noisily away in the direction of the street, trampling more expensive landscaping as he went.

There was more swearing from Barton as he came back in her direction, and softly called her name.

She stepped behind a tree, scarcely daring to breathe.

He walked within an arm's length of her, but she stayed still in the shadows and let him pass.

Barton released another quiet oath, and turned in the direction of the house, probably hoping to find her there.

She smiled in satisfaction. Let him look. She had the necklace again. There was no reason to stay a moment longer. It was not a chill night, she had no wrap. She could find her own way to the street through the garden, without taking leave of the host.

She turned into the darkness. At least she thought she could find her way to the street. If the house was behind her, then surely…

'Allow me.' A hand reached out of the darkness, and caught her arm.

She gasped. 'Smythe.'

'The same.'

'I thought you had gone.'

'And leave you alone in the dark? I think not. Do you have a carriage back at the house?'

'Barton sent a coach for me. I assumed that I would find a friend to escort me home.'

'And so you have. I will see you home, if you can leave immediately. I suspect I am no longer welcome in Barton's home.' She could see his grin in the darkness.

She smiled in return. 'And I have no wish to return. It suits me well.'

'Excellent.' It was impossible to tell, but he sounded sincerely pleased to have her company. He slipped his arm through hers and lead her in the direction of the street.

A thrill shot through her at the idea of being alone in the dark with him again, far from the safety of the house. Anything could happen and no one would be the wiser.

'You should not be so careless with your reputation, your Grace.'

'I beg your pardon?'

His voice was gentle, but held a hint of disapproval. 'You were alone in the garden. With Barton, I mean.'

'Only because you wished me to distract him,' she said acerbically. 'You left the method to me.'

'And I did not expect you to choose that one, after what you said to me as we danced. Did you wish for him to kiss you?'

'Not particularly.'

There was a hesitation. 'Did you enjoy it?'

'That is a very impertinent question.'

'And that is a very evasive answer.'

'But it is all you will get from me,' she said. 'Did you at least get what you were searching for?'

'No, I did not. And what makes you think I was searching for anything?'

She tipped her head to the side, considering. 'I am not sure. But I hope, if you merely intended burglary, you would not want or need to involve me in it.'

He nodded. 'That is true. And do not worry. It will not happen again. I have involved you too much already.'

'That is all right,' she said hurriedly. 'It was not too great a burden.'

'Allowing Barton to kiss you in the moonlight.' There was a cynical bite to his words that did not escape her.

'It was only a kiss,' she responded.

'Oh, really? But a kiss can be a dangerous thing, if done correctly.' He swung her body into his and wrapped his arms around her. 'Allow me to demonstrate.' And then he brought his mouth down upon hers.

It was as it had been on the night in her room. His kiss was as heady and romantic as the smell of the roses in the garden, and she relaxed into it, letting it awaken her senses.

She slipped her arms inside his coat, and felt the muscles of his back and shoulders tense as her fingers touched him. His arms strained to pull her closer to him, and he stroked her tongue with his, varying the pressure of his lips against hers from punishing firmness to a featherlight touch. When he released her mouth, she caught him about the waist and arched her body away from him, baring her throat and willing him to kiss her there, and lower.

He accepted the invitation and his lips trailed fire down her neck to rest on her shoulder. 'Do you enjoy it when *I* kiss you?' he murmured into her skin.

'Yes.' She shuddered against him.

He ran a finger inside the neckline of her gown and

pulled the dress away from her body, pushing to slide it down her arm. He planted a kiss just under the place where her dress should end, and she gasped.

He laughed and his finger traced her collarbone. 'I am going to kiss you there again. Hard enough to mark you. No one will know it but we two, because your gown will hide all. Would you like that?'

'Yes.' She shocked herself by saying it, knowing that it was true. 'Oh, yes.'

'I thought you might.' And he lowered his head again, and she felt him suck on the flesh, felt the feeling run through her all the way to her toes.

It was the work of a moment. And then it was over. He leaned his head against her ear and whispered, 'If you would kiss, then do not give them cheaply to one such as Barton. Choose someone worthy of your affection.' He walked her the last few steps through the trees and they came out at the bend of the drive. He whistled once and a carriage appeared from out of the darkness. Black and unmarked, with black horses and a driver muffled beyond recognition.

Smythe gave instructions to the driver and then he handed her up into the carriage, shutting the door behind her.

She leaned out of the window to where he stood in the road. 'Are you not coming as well?'

'My man will see you home.' There was hunger in

his eyes as he stared up into her face. 'You are safer with him tonight than alone in a carriage with me.'

'But how will you get home?' *And where is home? And are you alone there?* She was bursting with unasked questions.

He smiled at her, his face dim in the light from the carriage lamps. 'Never worry about me, your Grace. I have ways. Until we meet again.' He bowed to her as the carriage pulled away and he disappeared into the darkness behind her.

She leaned back into the squabs, her heart hammering in her chest. He had been right about the danger in a kiss. His were as intoxicating as anything served at the party, and as compelling as Barton's were not.

Perhaps what Barton accused her of was true. She was more than willing to bend the rules if she felt she would not be caught. And Mr Smythe would see to it that what they did was safe and in secret.

Perhaps it was no more than that. He was passionate, but solicitous of her reputation. Where other men wished to parade her fallen virtue as a trophy to their skills at seduction, with Smythe no one would know that they had been together. When he was done with her he would leave as quietly as he had come, moving through her life like a fish through water.

And when they parted tonight, he had not said goodbye. She could scarce control herself at the thought of seeing him again. She could still feel the kiss, hot and sinful, a brand on her shoulder to remind her of all the ways and places he might kiss her, should she allow it.

And why had she been so quick to agree? Was it because he had not asked at all?

Not at first, perhaps. But once he had started, he had asked her what would make her happy. He had not tried to negotiate her out of her honour, or worried that he was being outbid by some other man. He had not given her an ultimatum, or threatened her with shame or discovery.

He'd given her the first kiss as a sample of what was to come, and pointed out that he could give her even more pleasure, this instant, if she would allow him to. There had been no talk of bracelets or houses, or paying off her grocer and cutting back her staff. Or even what he wanted from her. He had kissed her again because he had wanted to, and because he had known she would like it more than she had when kissing Barton. Just a moment of shared bliss, and then he was gone.

She slipped her own fingers under the shoulder of her dress, imagining that his lips were still on her. He had said that she wouldn't be safe with him, and she imagined him climbing in beside her and pulling her close in the darkness of the cab. She would be alone and completely at his mercy. And his hands would roam freely over her body, taking everything he wanted from her.

As though it mattered. She never wanted to be safe again.

She shook her head to clear the fantasy and leaned her face to the open window, feeling the breeze in her hair. She glanced at the passing streets. The direction seemed right, but how would the driver be able to find her house? She had not heard Smythe tell him the address.

She turned and knelt on the seat, opening the connecting window between the carriage and the driver. 'I live on Grosvenor Square, just past—'

'I know the way, your Grace. Do not concern yourself.'

He had used her title. And over the sound of the horses, she thought she heard a trace of amusement in his voice. He knew of her. And he knew other things as well.

'Your master, Mr Smythe—have you known him long?'

There was no answer. And the driver tickled the horses with the tassel of his whip so that their speed increased.

He was loyal. Enough so as not to speak. And Smythe trusted him more than he did himself.

Then that answered the question. The man was no casual hire, but a trusted associate. A partner in crime, perhaps?

They were nearing her house, and she bit her lip in frustration. She knew nothing about Mr Smythe. He was not one of Barton's familiars. And she had been too careless when he had been introduced to her and had not paid attention. She had not even heard his Christian name.

The carriage pulled smoothly to a stop in front of her home. The driver hopped down from the seat and opened the door for her, taking her hand and guiding her to the ground.

She looked at him, not sure what to expect. His face was no longer shielded from her, and she found it plain and honest. Surprisingly friendly. He was gazing back at her with a frank curiosity that she should have found inappropriate in a servant, had she not wanted words with him.

She tried again. 'Please. About Mr Smythe. I know very little. Not his address. Or even his first name. If I should need to contact him…' It was all horribly bold of her. The words died away in her throat.

The driver stared at her for a long moment, in a way that was totally devoid of subservience. And then his shoulders rose and fell once in a way that was part shrug and part silent laugh. He rummaged in his pocket, and came out with a white pasteboard, glancing at it before handing it to her. 'His card, your Grace.'

She swallowed. 'Thank you.' She tried not to appear too eager, but snatched the card from his hand, and turned from him, concealing it in the bodice of her dress. And then she ran up the walk and into her house.

Once inside, she fled up the steps and into her room, shutting the door and reaching down the front of her dress to find the card, nestled close between her breasts.

'Anthony de Portnay Smythe. Anthony Smythe. Tony. Anthony.' She tried various versions of the name, tasting them, and enjoying the way they felt on her tongue.

Before Susan came to help her undress for bed, she looked for a place to secrete the card, finally slipping it under her pillow. She could not help smiling at the foolishness of it, as her maid undid the hooks of her gown. As a token of affection, a calling card was not much to speak of. And the man had not given it to her, after all. Perhaps he did not mean for her to know more of him.

Susan was undoing her stays and as she turned the maid gave the slightest gasp. The mark was there on her shoulder. 'Did you have a pleasant evening, your Grace? At Lord Barton's party?' The remark was off-hand, as though nothing unusual had sparked it.

'Most pleasant,' Constance answered, unable to resist a small sigh of pleasure.

'So I suspected.' Susan was faintly disapproving.

'Despite the presence of Lord Barton,' Constance corrected. 'The man continues to be quite odious. I do not plan to see him again.'

'I should hope not, your Grace.' This seemed to put the maid's fears to rest.

'Although there is another gentleman…' She hid her smile behind her hand.

Susan grinned back at her. 'If he puts such a sparkle in your eye, then he must be a most singular person.'

'But how is one to know, Susan,' she asked impulsively, 'what the intentions of a gentleman are? I have been wrong so many times in the past.'

'If he makes you happy, your Grace, perhaps it is time to think with your heart and not your head.'

The thrill of it ran through her. If she were to think with her heart, the choice would be easy. She wanted Anthony Smythe, and she could have him.

For now. Her mind brought it all crashing back down to earth. It was seductively pleasurable to think of Mr Smythe. And surely there was no harm in dreaming. But it would be a temporary solution at best. If she accepted any more purses from him, while allowing him to toy with her affections and use her body for his own pleasure, then she was little better than what she feared she would become.

But suppose he offered marriage?

The thought was as fascinating as it was horrifying. And not something that needed reckoning with. She would be a fool to trust him, or read too much into a few kisses. The first night, he had sworn that he loved another. He might be faithless to the other woman, and willing to dally with Constance for a while, if she encouraged him to. But in the end, his intentions to her would prove the same as all the others.

Although it might be more pleasurable with him,

than with others, for he was as passionate as he was considerate.

But he was a thief, she reminded herself. Even should she wish for an honourable union, there would be no way to overlook her lover's chosen occupation. A breath of the truth would destroy her reputation along with his. Eventually, he would be caught, and hanged, and she would be ruined in the bargain. Worse than she was now, alone, unloved and disgraced as well.

She shook her head sadly at Susan. 'Alas, I think I cannot afford to allow my heart to lead in this. The answer is not Barton, certainly. But it cannot be the other, no matter how much I might wish it so.' She allowed Susan to help her into bed and to blow out the candle, leaving her in the dim light of the fire, alone between the cold sheets.

And almost without thinking, her hand stole beneath the pillows and sought the calling card, running her fingers along the edge, feeling the smoothness of the pasteboard, and stroking the engraving as sleep took her.

Chapter Six

Patrick opened the bed curtains with more vehemence than necessary. Tony squinted as the late-morning sunlight hit him. And now his servant was rattling the plates on the breakfast tray. 'And a good morning to you too, Patrick,' he grumbled, reaching a hand out for his coffee. Patrick did not approve of the hour his master had gotten in, did he? Then he could go to the devil.

After sending his carriage away, Tony had enjoyed the excellent hospitality of the Earl of Stanton, given his regards to Lady Esme, and assured St John that he had been quite mistaken about the Duchess of Wellford. The woman was innocent.

In all the ways that mattered to the State. He smiled in satisfaction as he remembered the way she'd bitten her lip when he'd sucked on her shoulder, and dug her fingers into his sides to pull him closer. A certain lack of innocence in other areas might not be the worst thing.

But it had been embarrassing to stand before Stanton and admit his lack of success, when it came to the rest of the Barton matter. He could report on the location of the printing press in the basement, along with the inks and the paper. There was no evidence that printing of any false bills had occurred, but all the components needed were easily accessible. It would do him no good to destroy the supplies, other than to demonstrate to Barton that someone had tumbled to his plan. Tony needed to get the plates, and they were most likely locked tight in the safe in the study, behind a Bramah lock where he could not get to them.

St John had been most unimpressed with the gravity of the situation.

'Try again,' St John had said, pouring another whisky for his guest.

The fact that the Bramah lock was reported to be unpickable had little impact on his host. Had he never seen the challenge lock that Bramah displayed in their shop window, to taunt thieves and lockpicks? The company offered two hundred guineas to the first man who could open it. It had stood for more than twenty years so far, with no one able to claim the prize.

Stanton was too kind to suggest the return of the down payment, but Tony suspected it might enter the conversation if he belaboured the impossibility of the task before him.

He could afford to return the money and walk away, of course. But it stung his pride to think that such a thing might be necessary. It went against his grain to admit defeat, and although the impregnability of the lock was common knowledge, common knowledge was frequently wrong. It might take more time than was available to a burglar, but perhaps with practice…

He looked at Patrick, who was laying out his clothes for the day, and turned his mind to more pleasant matters. Willing his face to give nothing away, he said, 'The return trip to the Wellford house was uneventful, I trust.'

Patrick finished brushing his coat before responding. 'A stray cat almost met an unfortunate end beneath the carriage wheels, but I was able to prevent disaster.'

'And the duchess arrived home safely?'

'To her very door. She was a most grateful, and, you will forgive me for noticing, sir, a most attractive passenger.'

Patrick approved. It was strangely pleasing to have his opinion of Constance confirmed by his valet.

'Although strangely talkative, for nobility,' Patrick continued. 'Most of the peerage can't be bothered…'

'Talkative?'

'Yes, sir.' Patrick returned to the choosing of shirts as if nothing important had been said.

When Tony could stand it no longer, he asked, 'And what did she say?'

'She asked after you, sir.'

'After me.' Tony sat up, almost spilling his coffee in the process.

'Indeed, sir.' Patrick set the rest of the breakfast tray in front of him, refilled the coffee cup and stepped away.

'And what did you tell her?'

'I didn't think it my place, sir.'

The man picked the damnedest times to remember his station and to behave as a servant.

'I assumed you must have had a reason for neglecting to mention your Christian name, or to give her your direction. Perhaps you had no wish to be troubled by the lady again.'

Tony groaned, and wiped his face with his hands. She did not know who he was? He'd been formally introduced to her, for God's sake.

And she had had eyes only for Barton. Tony stabbed his kipper with more force than necessary.

Patrick brightened. 'And then I realised what a great ninny you are around women, and more so with a certain woman in particular. And I suspected that you had merely forgotten the importance of the information. So I gave her one of your cards.'

Tony slumped in relief. 'And how did she receive it?'

Patrick mimed putting a calling card down the front

of an imaginary dress. 'I dare say your good name has got further with the lady than you have yourself.'

Later, as Patrick shaved him, Tony could feel his face, set in a ridiculous grin. She'd wanted to know his name. And carried it next to her…heart.

The image of the card nestling against her body, warmed by her skin, made him almost dizzy with desire. Patrick was right, he should capitalise on the situation immediately. He rubbed a finger experimentally along his jaw line. Smooth. Not that she had complained the night before. But it would not do to let her think he took her interest for granted. 'Patrick, my best suit, please, I am going out. And extra care with the cravat, please.'

'Yes, sir.'

'And while I am gone, Patrick, I have a task that needs doing. Please go down to the Bramah Locks Company. I wish a safe installed in my study. Fitted with one of their fine locks. The job must be rushed, for I have valuables to store, and am most afraid of thieves.'

'Yes, sir.'

Two hours later, Tony had to admit that the day was not going to plan. He had imagined a quiet chat with Constance, in her sitting room. Kissing in the moonlight was all well and good. Much better than good, to be truthful. But he must make some attempt to assure her that in daylight he was not without the manners of a common gentleman, if their association was to go any further.

He ignored the novelty of it, and called at the front door, but was disappointed to find her Grace was not at home. He left a card and enquired of the butler, as politely as possible, where she might be on such a fine day.

And now he found himself frequenting the lending library in Bond Street, hoping to catch sight of her as she ran her errands. When she entered, he was paging though a volume of poems that he had read a hundred times, trying to appear the least bit interested in contents that he could barely see, since his reading glasses were at home in his desk.

And she was not alone, damn the luck. There was a man at her side who gave every indication of solicitous interest, and two young ladies as well.

What was he to do? In the scenario he'd imagined, she'd been shopping alone, or perhaps with her maid to carry packages. It would be easy to approach her and he would make some offhand remark that might make reference to the evening before without mentioning it directly.

She would laugh, and respond. He would offer to carry her books. She would graciously accept. Conversation would ensue. He would let slip certain facts, recognition would dawn in her eyes, and he would be spared the embarrassment of having to reintroduce himself to a woman who had known him since they were both three.

Nowhere in his plan had he considered that the position of book carrier and witty conversationalist might already be occupied. Tony could not very well pretend not to see her, and she could not help but notice him, for he'd positioned himself in such a way as to be unavoidable.

Damn it to hell, but he must speak to her.

He turned and took a step towards her, just as she made to go past. And in the second before he spoke, he caught her eye as it tried to slide past without meeting his. There was alarm, followed by embarrassment, and finally resignation, before she managed to choose an expression to suit the situation—a friendly smile that said to the people around her, I think I know this man, but am unsure.

It was too late. The words were already out of his mouth. 'Your Grace. A most lovely day, is it not?'

'Why, yes. Yes, it is. Mr…'

'Smythe, ma'am. We met at Lord Barton's party last evening.' The words sounded false, but she leapt on them as salvation.

'Why, of course. How foolish of me. Mr Smythe, may I introduce Viscount Endsted and his sisters, Catherine and Susanne.'

'Ladies. Your lordship.' He made his best bow, and was dismayed to hear the ladies giggle in appreciation.

When his eyes rose to Constance, he saw fresh

alarm there at the young ladies' reaction. He was not suitable for them, either. Once he had gone, she would have to warn them off.

'Mr Smythe.' There was a slight emphasis on the mister, and the Viscount took a step forward to head off the interested sisters and gripped his hand.

His handshake was firm to an almost painful degree. Tony considered, for a moment, the advantage to responding in kind, then discarded it as infantile.

As the viscount sensed him yield, he released his grip as well. Endsted glanced at the book in Tony's hand. 'Byron?'

'Yes. I find it—' How did he find it? He did not wish to give the wrong answer and further jeopardise his position with Constance. 'Most edifying.'

Endsted's sisters giggled, and Endsted glared at them. 'The man's scandalous. I do not hold with him. Not in the least.'

'I have no real opinion of the man,' Tony responded, 'for I have never met him. But his poetry is in no way morally exceptionable.' He glanced to Constance.

She looked as though she would rather cut out her tongue than have an opinion. Endsted was glaring at her, waiting for her to agree.

'He is rather fast,' she managed. She flashed a brief, hopeless look in Tony's direction, before looking to Endsted for approval.

Endsted nodded. 'His works are not fit for a lady.'

Which showed how little the man knew of ladies or of poetry, Tony suspected. 'I do not know, sir. I find his skill with words to be an excellent tribute for certain ladies.'

Constance pretended to ignore the compliment, but he could see a faint flush at the neck of her gown.

'But not something one might wish to speak of in a lending library.'

Tony chose to ignore the man's disapproval and answered innocently, 'For myself, I should think there would be no better place to discuss books.'

'I suppose it is a way to pass the time for one who has nothing better to do than read poetry.' He said the last words as if reading were one step from taking opium with Lord Byron himself. 'And now, sir, if you will excuse us.' He took Constance by the arm and led her past.

She did not look back, although the Endsted sisters cast a backward glance in his direction, giggling again.

Tony debated calling the man back to argue poetry, morality and general manners, or planting him a facer and reading works by the scandalous Lord Byron over his prone body, then thought the better of it. He doubted demonstrating Endsted's ignorance would win him points in the eyes of Constance, and might endear him further to the man's sisters, which was a fate to be avoided.

And he had no evidence that there was any behaviour that might find favour with Constance. At least, in the light of day. There was no question that she responded to him in the dark. And she did so in a way that made it very hard for him to wish to remove himself totally from her company.

But it appeared likely that, should he continue to meet with her, he would spend evenings losing all reason in her passionate embrace, only to be replaced at the breakfast table by a viscount and his giggling sisters. And really, if she wanted to marry another peer, then who was he to stand in her way? She had her own future to attend to, and, if he loved her, he must accept the fact that it was not in her best interest to associate with him.

All in all, his life had been much easier before he'd climbed in her window. His nights had been lonely and his passion had been hopeless. But he had made peace with that years ago. Now, the only hope he had of a return to peace was to put all thoughts of Constance Townley aside, and spend evenings in quiet communion with his lockpicks and his new safe.

He set the book back on a nearby shelf, and yielded the field to the better man.

Chapter Seven

'Lemon?' Constance arranged the tea things, for the hundredth time, trying to ignore Endsted's growing irritation with her.

'No, thank you.' Looking at the sour expression on the viscount's face, she suspected he had no need of any additional bitterness. She offered the sugar, instead.

She offered each, in turn, to his two sisters, and they helped themselves, casting sidelong glances at her last, uninvited tea guest.

When there was no one else to serve, she turned to him, and repeated her offer in a tone that she hoped would tell him to take his tea and go to the devil.

'Thank you.' Jack Barton smiled as though there was nothing unusual in her voice, took the lemon she offered, and set it at the side of his saucer.

She felt his fingers brush hers, and silently cursed.

She had been too slow to move, and he had managed to arrange the accidental touch.

And Endsted had noticed. He was an annoyingly observant man. He was also upright, noble and extremely respectable, if a bit of a prig. But he was the first man whose company she had shared who was clear in his willingness to introduce her to his family. His intentions were honourable, or he'd never have allowed her to meet his sisters.

And she had managed to disappoint him, first with Mr Smythe, now with Barton, who had been waiting in her sitting room when they'd returned from the library, uninvited and unmoving.

And Susan had made her day even more of a disaster, by whispering that, while Lord Barton had taken up residence despite her encouragement that waiting would not be welcome or convenient, Mr Smythe had been most co-operative and departed after enquiring of her whereabouts.

So Smythe had been hoping to see her when they'd met in the library. She had feared as much. From a distance, he'd appeared to be the poised and confident man that she'd seen at the ball the previous evening.

But as she'd approached him, she'd seen an eagerness in his manner that she had not seen in a man in… How long had it been? Since she'd had suitors, well before Robert. Long ago, when those who sought her affections had had hopes of success and fears of disappointment. There had been none of the sly looks and innuendos that accompanied all interactions with men now that she was a widow.

Tony Smythe had looked at her as though the years had meant nothing, and she was a fresh young girl with more future than responsibilities. And she had crushed him by her indifference.

She had feared, last night, that there would be nothing to speak of, should she see him in daylight. But today she had found him reading Byron.

She adored Byron.

She looked across the table at Endsted, and remembered that he found Byron most unsuitable. If she succeeded with him, there would be no more poetry in her life. She could spend her evenings reading educational and enlightening tracts to Endsted's rather foolish sisters.

She looked to her other side, at Lord Barton. Surely a boring life with Endsted would be preferable to some fates.

Of course, Mr Smythe would read Byron to her. In bed, if she asked him to. Or would have done, had she not set him down in public to secure her position with Endsted. She doubted she would be seeing him again.

And why was she thinking of him at all, when she needed to keep her mind on her guests? She dragged her attention back to managing the men in front of her. Silence between them was long and cold on Endsted's side. It appeared he had heard the rumours of Barton's character and was only suffering contact with him out of straining courtesy to Constance.

Barton did not seem to mind the frigid reception. He ignored Endsted and smiled at the ladies. 'Might I remark, Lord Endsted, on the attractiveness of your sisters.'

Endsted glared and the girls giggled.

'I cannot remember a day when I have been so fortunate as to find myself in the company of so many charming young ladies.' He focused his gaze for more than a little too long on the eldest, Catherine, until she coloured and looked away.

'Are you a friend of Constance's?' the girl asked timidly.

'Oh, a most particular friend,' Barton answered.

Constance could not very well deny it while the man was in her parlour, sipping her tea. She dare not explain, in front of her other guests, that she allowed him there only because of the things he might say to them about her, should she try to have him removed.

'Yes,' Barton repeated, 'I am a friend of her Grace, and would like to be your friend as well, should your brother allow it. Might I have permission to call upon you tomorrow?'

'Most certainly not.' Endsted's composure snapped, and he rose from the table. 'Catherine, Susanne. We are leaving.'

The girls did not like the command, but they responded quickly, and rose as well. He shepherded them towards the door, and turned back to Barton and Constance. 'I know your measure, sir, as does the rest of decent society. And I'll thank you to give my family a wide berth in the future. If I catch you dangling after my sisters again, we will settle this on the field of honour and not in a drawing room.'

And then he turned to Constance, and there was disappointment, mingling with his anger. 'I cannot know what you were thinking, to allow him here. If you will not be careful of your guests, Constance, at least have a care for yourself.' And with a final warning glance, he left the room.

She turned back to the tea table, where Barton had returned to his seat, and his cup. She stood above him, hands planted on hips, and he had not even the courtesy to rise for her. The insults and the threats from Endsted had had no effect on his composure, either. He had the same serene smile as when she'd returned home to find him waiting.

'There,' Constance snapped. 'Endsted has gone, and I doubt he will return. I hope you are satisfied.'

Barton looked at her, and his gaze was so possessive and familiar that she wished she could strike him. He stared as if he could see through her clothes. 'Not totally. But I expect I soon will be.'

'If that was some pitiful attempt at a *double entendre*, you needn't bother.'

'Oh, really, it is no bother. In fact, I quite enjoy it.'

She shuddered in revulsion. 'You horrible, horrible man. I do not care how you feel about it. I do not enjoy it. I find it offensive. It is vile. I cannot make it any plainer than that. I do not want you, or your rude comments. If you persist in your pursuit of me, my response will be the same as it was the last time: I do not want you. I will not want you. I never want to see you again. Now get out of my house.' By the time she was finished, she was shouting.

'Your house?' He smiled and his tone never wavered.

And, suddenly, she knew that he knew about the loss of the deed and she also had a horrible suspicion about its current ownership.

'I believe you are mistaken,' he continued, 'about this being your house. If it were yours, you would be able to show me the deed, would you not?'

He knew. He had to. But if there was even the smallest chance that she was wrong, she would keep up the pretence. 'I do not have it here. It is in the bank, where it can be kept safe.'

'Is it, now?' He wagged a finger at her. 'I think, Constance, that you are not telling me the whole truth. It is far more likely that your nephew had the deed in his keeping, not wishing to give up his power over you so easily. He is not the best card player, even when sober. And he is rarely sober, Constance. Quite likely to gamble away his estate.' He smiled coldly. 'Not his estate, perhaps. When one loses enough in a night to equal the cost of one's townhouse…well, one might as well lose the cost of another house instead.'

'He didn't.'

'I'm afraid he did. The deed is safe enough. I have it in my possession. Would you like to give me a tour of my property? We could begin upstairs.'

'I do not believe you,' she stalled.

'Then you must go to the duke and ask him. It must be very trying for you to have your future in the hands of such an idiot.'

She grasped at her last hope. 'Freddy cannot legally give away what is not his. I will appeal to the courts. It is my house. My name is on the deed.'

Barton shrugged. 'Now, perhaps. But it does not take much talent to change a few lines of ink. By the time anyone sees the paper, I will be sure it says what I wish it to say. You will find, Constance, that the courts will want proof. You will have your word, of course. But I will have evidence. If you have any doubts, you can ask Freddy what he has to say on the matter.'

Too late to pretend, then. 'Lord Barton…' she began hesitantly. 'I have already been to see the duke, and he has explained to me what has become of the house.'

Barton nodded, still smiling.

She swallowed. 'And I assume that there will be a rent set, now that I am your tenant.'

He was enjoying her discomposure. 'You know that it is not money that I want from you.'

She closed her eyes in defeat. 'Then I will be out of the house by morning.'

He grabbed her wrist and her eyes snapped open at the shock of the unwelcome contact. 'Not so fast, my dear. I understand it is fully furnished. There is an attached inventory. If you can assure me that everything is in its proper place, we can dispense with the tour.'

She wet her lips. He knew that her furniture had gone the way of her jewels. There was no point in pretending it had not.

'There is an easier way, you know. You stay in the house. You keep the servants and I give you enough money to replace all that you have taken, even the stones in the rest of your jewellery. But you accept the fact that it is my house that you live in, and I will come and go, and do as I please when here. And no door will be barred to me.'

The hand on her wrist relaxed into a gentle grip. 'It is not an unpleasant proposition I am making, I assure you. I am not a cruel man. My mistresses have always found me to be generous and they assure me I am good company. But I do not like to be opposed.'

'And I do not like to be forced.'

'You are not being forced. You have options. You can leave the house and its contents intact. Then there will be no reason for me to call the law to retrieve my property. Or you can accept that you are my guest here, and treat me with the gratitude I deserve for solving so many of your problems. I will give you two days to consider the matter. That should be enough time to put your house in order.'

He snapped his fingers. 'Correction. My house in order. I will return on Monday, Constance. At that time, you will give me the keys. Whether you stay or go is completely up to you. Until then.' And he bent his head to hers and kissed her.

She wished that it had been a repellent kiss, and that she had fought it, as one would fight untimely death. But instead, she closed her eyes and leaned into him, opening her mouth and trying to remember what it had been like to kiss Robert so.

She had to admit the truth to herself: Barton was not unskilled at kissing. If it were not Barton holding her, the experience would not be unpleasant. He did a creditable job of trying to arouse her passions.

She imagined she was in Tony's arms, and she did a creditable job of pretending to be aroused. And so it was likely to be from now on.

'That was not so very bad, was it?'

Her voice quavered as she spoke, and she could feel a flush of shame on her face. 'We are not finished here, Jack. Do not think that you have won.'

'We can discuss my chances of victory on Monday, Constance. Until then.'

And he left her there, trembling with rage. It was one thing to sell one's dreams to get a husband. If there was no promise of love, then at least there was a guarantee of security until such time as the fool man had to go and die, leaving one's future in the hands of his idiot nephew…

She shook her head. She would not let Barton use her at his will, and cast her off when he tired of her. There had to be another way. If she had the deed and the inventory, then the house would be hers. She would put it somewhere safe, out of the hands of Freddy and all others, as she should have done from the first. There would be no further discussion.

But Barton was not likely to give it to her just because she wanted it. He would make her earn it. If she wanted it, then she must find a way to take it from him. She imagined sneaking into his house in the night, and rifling his desk. He would keep it somewhere he could look at it and admire his cleverness, much as he planned to keep her on display in her own house.

All she need do was go to his house under cover of darkness, find the deed, and steal away with it without anyone noticing. An impossibility. Even if she could get past the locked door, she doubted she would have the nerve necessary to take the thing.

But she knew someone with nerve enough for both of them. Her heart skipped at the memory of him climbing boldly out of her window and down to the ground as silently as a shadow. And he had been in the study before. He might even know where to look.

If she could make him do it for her. She had done what he wished at the previous night's ball. He had said that would clear any debt she might owe, with regards to the money he had left her. And she had allowed him to kiss her in the garden. But she had hurt him, too, in the circulating library. What reason could he possibly have to help her, after that?

The same reason everyone else had to offer her assistance. He, at least, had made a more interesting proposition when he'd made her pay him back. And he'd left her with hard currency to trade.

And, she had to admit it, a certain willingness to barter. Did she seriously plan to sell her honour so cheaply?

She thought of the single kiss in the moonlight, and the way her body had responded as they'd danced. She was hardly selling herself cheap if it was a house she gained. And it was not as if she would need feign too hard, when the moment came to give all. It might be quite pleasant to lie back and let him have his way.

She flushed. Her current fantasy of what might happen when next she was alone with Anthony Smythe had very little to do with passive submission to his advances. She must take care or her response, when the moment came, was likely to be aggressive to an unladylike degree.

But to the matter at hand, how did one go about offering oneself in exchange for services?

She shuddered. That was what she was planning to do. And it did no good to paint the act in romantic fantasies, even if the experience proved as pleasant as it was likely to. Any relationship they might have after tonight would be in fulfilment of a transaction and not the passionate idyll she'd created in her imagination.

She sighed. If life were dreams, it would not be as it had been in the library, today. She would have come upon Mr Smythe when she was alone, and he would ply her with poetry and promises of discretion. They would meet in secret, and he would grow bolder with each meeting. She would put up a token display of resistance before succumbing to his considerable romantic skills. Their inevitable parting would be bittersweet, but she would have a memory that she could carry into whatever cold future awaited her.

But now, she must forgo romance and throw herself on the mercy of the thief, or she would be spending her immediate future in the company of Lord John Barton. Nothing was lost, she reminded herself. Neither path led to a likelihood of slow seduction by Anthony Smythe, but one was infinitely more pleasant, once she got over the initial distaste of being so forward as to make the first move.

And if she was to move, there was no time to waste. She hurried up the stairs to her room and called for her maid. 'Susan?'

'Yes, your Grace.'

'I am going out. The gold dress, I think.' It was attractive on her, she thought. And she wished to look her best. Susan helped her into the gown and Constance appraised herself in the pier glass.

She had always thought this her most lovely gown, but now she was not so sure. It was grand, certainly. The gold threads caught the candlelight, and tiny beads glittered in the poufs of white satin that trimmed it, and weighted the skirt. But it seemed too stiff and formal for what she had in mind this particular evening.

She wanted to be beautiful for him. A prize worthy of any risk he might take to achieve it. But she did not want to seem unapproachable. How best to make the point clear? She took a deep breath to steady herself, and then she said, 'Susan, help me out of these stays.'

Her maid's eyes widened in alarm. 'You are not going to see Lord Barton again, are you, your Grace?'

'I should think not, Susan. I know someone who might be willing to help on that account, if I ask him nicely.' And with no stays, she would not have to ask aloud.

The maid nodded. 'Very good, ma'am.' Susan removed the dress, helped her out of her corset and tossed the dress back over her head.

The effect was startling. While the fabric was not sheer, it clung to her body, heavy with the weight of the beads. She could almost see the outline of her breasts inside the dress.

And if she could see them, so could he.

She swallowed. Very well. At least there would be no misunderstanding. It needed but one thing to complete the effect. She closed her eyes in embarrassment. 'Susan? How does one damp one's skirts?'

'Your Grace?' Her maid gave an incredulous giggle.

'I've heard of it's being done, but I don't think I've ever actually seen it…'

Chapter Eight

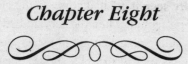

The evening found her shivering inside her cloak, waiting for Mr Smythe to enter his study. Constance had discovered the reason, firsthand, why the practice of dampened petticoats had never caught on. She had thought it was the extreme immodesty that prevented popularity. But now that she had tried it, she suspected it had as much to do with the discomfort involved. The fabric was cold and wet against her body, and she thought she was as likely to catch her death as catch a man because of it.

But the image presented when she saw herself in the mirror might be most effective, if the object of the evening was seduction. The thin fabric of the skirt clung to her legs and outlined her hips and belly. Without the troublesome stays, her breasts rested soft and full in the bodice of her dress, and tightened in response to the chill of the skirts. The rouge on her cheeks and lips was subtle, but made her mouth look kissable in the candlelight. There was no trace left of the aloof duchess to obscure the vulnerable and desirable woman she saw there.

When she'd arrived at Smythe's rooms, she'd almost lost her nerve, and had clung to the cloak as her last line of protection when the servant had offered to take it. It would be hard enough to shed, once the object of her mission was in sight, and she meant to keep it as long as she could.

At last, Smythe stepped into the room, and she turned to greet him.

He smiled politely. 'Your Grace? To what do I owe the honour of this visit?'

She let the cloak slip from her shoulders and drop to the floor around her.

There was a long pause, as he took in her appearance. And then, he said, 'Oh.' And his face went blank.

She waited, but no response was forthcoming. He stood, rooted to the spot, silent and staring at her as though he did not quite understand what he was seeing.

Dear God, what had she done? She had assumed that she recognised his interest. And he had kissed her. Twice. But perhaps he was thus with all women when he was alone with them.

It had been the servant who had given her the direction to this place, not Mr Smythe. She had not thought, before coming here, to question whether he wished to entertain her in his home. He had certainly never invited her to it. After the afternoon in the library, he might not wish to see her at all, much less see her nearly naked in his study.

He might have other plans for the evening. He might not be alone. Worse yet, he might be married, although there was nothing about the rooms to indicate the fact. And she had blundered forward, dressed like a courtesan and expecting a warm greeting.

She stared down at the cloak on the floor, willing it to jump back into place around her shoulders, and then she looked back at Mr Smythe.

He was still staring at her, taking in every detail. He forgot himself and sat down. And then sprang from his chair, and motioned to her. 'Please, sit. May I offer you a drink? Tea?'

She sank gratefully on to a nearby settee. 'Sherry?'

'Of course.' She noted the speed with which he summoned a servant, and the eagerness of his voice. He did not let his man come fully into the room, blocking the entrance with his body and taking the tray from him at the door. Then he returned to her, busying himself with the pouring of wine as though he did not know what to do with his hands.

Did this mean he was still interested in her? Or had she embarrassed him in some way? Until he spoke, it was difficult to tell. But whatever he felt, it wasn't anger, for he showed no sign of turning her out, and he'd have done it by now, surely.

He offered her a glass, but still said nothing. She took her sherry and sipped, crossing her legs, and watching as he watched the movement of her skirt and swallowed some of his own wine.

At last she could stand the silence no longer. All the witty conversational gambits she'd imagined had involved two people who were capable of speech. There would be no clever sparring around the truth, or coy avoidance if she could not get Tony to respond beyond a monosyllable. Finally she gave up and went directly to the reason for her visit, without preamble. 'I need your help.'

'Anything,' he breathed. And then he remembered to look into her eyes. He cleared his throat, and his face went blank again, as he pretended that he had not just been trying to stare through her clothes. When he spoke, his voice had returned to its normal tone. 'How may I assist you? I am at your service.'

Very well. He wished to pretend that there was nothing unusual about her appearance? Then so would she. She stared unflinchingly into his eyes. 'I need something taken. Stolen, from another person.' Her nerve began to falter. 'It was mine to begin with, so in a sense, it is not stealing at all.'

His voice hardened, as he responded. 'Do not justify. I trust that you would never ask this of me if the reason were not a good one. You need something taken? Then I am your man. Direct me to it.'

'Jack Barton has the deed to my house. My house, mind you. Not my husband's or my nephew's. It was promised to me.' She heard the whine in her voice, and took a deep breath. 'I assume you can guess the reason why he might wish to keep it. It is very economical on his part to allow me to remain in my own house, in exchange for my hospitality when he visits me there. He needn't even let some rooms.'

She was pleased to see the murderous look on the face of Mr Smythe as the situation sunk in.

'And I would like to have it back. But I am not sure where he might be keeping it.'

'That is all right,' he said hurriedly. 'I have a pretty good idea of its location. It was a rum trick to play on you, and I have no objection to settling the score. I'll fix the bastard so that he's ill inclined to try it again.' He seemed almost relieved not to have to think about her, and his eyes lost focus as he began to plan the job. 'The thing will take several days, but you must be patient and allow me to know what is best in this matter. I will bring the deed to you as soon as I have it safely away.'

'I need it before Monday. That is when he means to…take occupancy.'

His attention snapped back to the present, and he was aware of her again. There was a long pause, and for a moment, she feared that he was about to retract his offer of help. Then he said, 'Monday? This is not an easy thing you are asking. But I understand that your need is urgent. I will adjust my own plans so that I may help you. You will have it by Monday.'

'Thank you.'

There was another long silence. She had expected that this was where he would explain to her the cost of the service, and she took another sip of the sherry, wetting her lips to agree, when he asked.

But he said nothing. He just continued to gaze at her, watching her lips as she drank the sherry, scanning slowly down to admire her breasts, making no effort to clarify her position. She could feel her skin grow warm under his gaze, and her nipples tightening.

At last she could no longer stand the silence. She stared down into her wine glass and said, 'If you were to do this for me, I would be very grateful. Once it is done, of course. Once the item is returned to me, there is nothing that you would ask that I would refuse.'

'Nothing,' he said flatly.

'Nothing,' she affirmed.

'Anything I might think to ask in payment, any request I might make, you would be willing to comply?'

She ignored the heat rising in her. 'Yes.'

His voice dropped to a sensuous murmur, and she could feel the words dancing along her nerves. 'Be warned, I have an extremely vivid imagination.'

Suddenly, so did she. She closed her eyes tight and

the fantasies that rose at the sound of his voice became more intense. Her blood sizzled as she imagined what it might be like to submit to the whims of a man who was little more than a stranger—a hardened criminal, accustomed to taking what he wanted. 'Anything you wish.'

'But what will you say in the morning, I wonder?' His voice had returned to normal again.

'I have no idea what you mean,' she responded, a little too easily.

'I should think it's obvious. It was to me, at least. I am not good enough to be seen with, when you are in the presence of your friends. It is much safer here, is it not, where there is no one you know?'

The words stung her. 'And how could I have introduced you to Endsted?' she retorted. 'This is Mr Smythe. We met in my bedroom, when he was stealing my jewellery. Really, Tony, you ask the impossible of me.'

'Tony, is it, now? I had no idea, your Grace, that we had progressed to that level of familiarity. I suppose I should be flattered. When you meet me in the future, you may call me whatever you choose. You need not mention knowing me in my professional capacity at all. We have been introduced at a formal gathering, although you did not pay a great deal of attention at the time. You have danced with me. We have made polite conversation. I had hoped that you might be able to treat me as you treat others. And as I have treated you: with courtesy and respect.'

'Courtesy and respect? That is beyond enough. You have taken liberties with my person.'

'I apologise,' he responded stiffly. 'I rather thought, at the time, that you enjoyed them. And if I do not miss my guess, you just invited to do as I pleased with you. But if I was mistaken, and have been taking unwelcome liberties, then I humbly apologise. It will not happen again.'

Her anger faded, as she remembered how he'd looked in the library. She had hurt him with her snub. And now she had come to his rooms to hurt him again. She could feel the cool air passing through her gown, fighting back the heat in her skin. She was being utterly shameless, trying to trap Tony into helping her. And yet she was berating him for his behaviour. She looked down at the designs her toe was tracing in the rug. 'I mis-spoke. You have not taken anything from me that was not freely offered. But Barton came to my rooms after we spoke this afternoon. And in my panic, I could not think where else to turn. I thought, after the kiss in the garden, you would not be averse to my offer tonight.'

He laughed. 'Oh, your Grace, I'm not averse. Not in the slightest. Especially with you dressed like that.' He stared at her body, making no effort to hide his interest. Finally, he gave a deep sigh of satisfaction. 'Say the word and I'll have you on the hearthrug, right now, and make sure you don't regret the offer. But understand, if I wished to be compensated for my services, I would request payment in full, up front of the job.' He stared into her eyes and his smile faded. 'With the risks I'm taking, I never withhold pleasure or payment for tomorrow. One can not guarantee the outcome. If they catch me and hang me, your gratitude is worthless.'

'Very well, then.' Here and now? He would not even lead her to his bed? She felt her knees turn to water and a tremor of excitement go through her at the thought of what was about to happen. She reached to undo her bodice, trying not to rush in her eagerness.

'I did not request payment.'

Her hand stopped.

'When did I ever demand anything of you?' he asked softly. 'I said I would do this for you, and I shall. I do not wish to—how did you put it?—"take liberties". From you, I do not wish to take anything at all. I will take care of your problem.' He waved his hand as though dealing with Barton were no more difficult than shooing a fly. 'Tonight, all you needed to do was ask and I would have offered to do all in my power to aid you. And as a gentleman, I do not require your gratitude afterwards. Do not mention it again.'

'Thank you.' But she did not feel like thanking him. She felt like shouting at him. And the flush in her cheeks was from shame, not excitement.

There was another long pause. And his eyes remained focused on her face, studiously ignoring the rest of her. 'Is there anything else you wished of me?'

There were many things, none of which she could very well ask for. To begin with, she wanted him to gaze at her as he had done, when she had entered the room, and not with the coldness and disdain he was showing now. 'No, I think that is all.'

He nodded, and said nothing more. His expression did not change. The silence stretched between them.

'I should probably be going, then.'

He nodded. 'I think that's best. Do you wish me to escort you home?' And now he showed the same level of concern that any gentleman might show to a lady.

'No. I am all right. It was not far to walk.' She could not stand the embarrassment of his respect a moment longer.

'You walked?' His voice held disapproval. 'It is not seemly or safe for a woman to travel alone at night. I will tell Patrick to get you a hackney.'

'No.' She had shocked him, by her behaviour, by coming alone to his home, and by her dress, or lack thereof. This was not how the night was to end at all.

'I insist.' His voice was emphatic, so she nodded and rose. He reached for her cloak and dropped it on to her shoulders, concealing her body from view before opening the door. She reached to pull it closed in front of her.

He escorted her to the door of his study and out into

the hall. He directed his servant to find her transportation. Then he turned his back upon her and returned to his room.

The servant whom she had met the previous night led her down the stairs and left her standing at the front door, as he hailed a cab for her, and she sensed pity in his smile as he helped her into the coach.

Anthony returned to his chair and waited until the door closed behind her, and then waited a little longer. He imagined her progress through the house and out of the front door. Then he drained his wine in a gulp, and called for his valet.

The man appeared like a ghost behind him. 'Sir?'

'Patrick, bring me brandy. And plenty of it.'

'Yes, sir.' Patrick was resigned to his master's behaviour, even if he did not approve of it. He left the room and reappeared a short time later, carrying a tray laden with a full bottle of the best brandy in the cellars.

Patrick poured the first glass, and when he seemed to be finished, his master signalled him with a raising of the hand. 'Eh, eh, eh, a little more, still.' Tony watched the level rise in the glass. He held up a hand. 'Stop. That's the ticket. And keep them coming, Patrick.' He drank half the brandy and blurted, 'That woman. I swear, Patrick, she will be the death of me. I cannot countenance what she did, just now.' He finished the glass, and held it out to be refilled.

'First she snubs me in public, and makes it known to me that she prefers another. Then she comes to me, soft and willing, just as I've always dreamed she would. She is finally here, and wants my help. And at any time, does she recognise me? No.'

'It has been a long time, sir. Both you and she have changed significantly.'

'One thing has not changed. She did not want me then, and she does not want me now. Did you see her? Dear God.' He allowed himself a moment of carnal pleasure at the memory. 'No stays, thin silk gown, and I swear she'd damped the skirts.' He shook his head. 'Like a French woman. Nothing left to imagination, not that my imagination needs any help when it comes to her. But she should not have been out in the streets in that condition. She'd catch her death. She made it quite clear, in the library today, that she wanted no part of me, and that our association was an embarrassment.

'Very well. I do not need to be told twice. I meant to avoid her in the future. If she does not want me, then there is no point in making an even greater fool of myself than I have been.' He stared down into his second brandy. He was already feeling the effects of the first, and thought the better of the second drink, tossing the contents of the glass into the fire, listening to the spirits hissing in the flames.

'A few hours pass, and she comes to my room dressed to seduce me. Very well, thinks I. She has no trouble acknowledging me when we are alone. If I had any pride, I would refuse her. Which would prove I'm an even bigger fool than I thought, for how can I turn down an offer like this? She's been married long enough to know what's what and widowed long enough to miss it. She might ignore me tomorrow, but the morning is a long way off, and we'll have a time of it tonight.'

He stared down into his empty glass, and Patrick shook his head and poured again.

'And why did she come to me? She wants me to steal for her. Not a problem, of course. I'd die for her, if she but asked. Burglary is not a sticking point. And if I did, she would deign to lie with me. Afterwards. In gratitude.' He closed his eyes and drank more slowly this time.

'She looked at me with those sherry-coloured eyes, and hung her head as though the path to my bed was a passage to Botany Bay.' He finished the brandy and said sadly, 'It was not the way I'd imagined it.'

Patrick looked at him in disappointment. 'What you have wanted for half your life was here, within your grasp. And you choose instead to send it away and call for a brandy bottle.'

'It wasn't what I wanted,' he argued. 'Her gratitude, indeed.'

'What, exactly, do you want from her, then, if not to lie with her?'

'I want her to see me for who I am, even if she cannot see me for who I was. All she sees is the thief, Patrick. And to catch him, she was willing to be the whore that a thief deserved.' He thought back to the sight of her, her breasts swaying beneath her gown, her legs outlined by the cloth. 'Not that I minded, seeing her. But I wager she does not dress thusly when she is trying to impress Endsted.'

'Would you wish her to, sir?'

'No. Of course not. If it were my choice, she would not see Endsted, again, under any circumstances. And I would make damn sure that he never got to see what I saw tonight. The man is an utter prig. I doubt he'd have known what to do with her, in any case.'

'Unlike you, sir, Endsted would have sat there like a lecher, staring at her charms while making it clear that he disapproved of her behaviour. And then he would have insulted her by sending her away. She would have gone home, with head hung low and near tears, convinced that she was in some way morally repellent or deformed in body. I am sure she will think twice in the future before exposing to the gentleman in question any sign of interest or vulnerability that might lead to further ridicule.'

Tony ignored the dark look that Patrick was giving him, to drive the point home. 'You're saying I should go to her, then. Apologise.'

Patrick nodded. 'Because there is nothing that will

make amends better than appearing on her doorstep after half a bottle of brandy, and trying to say the things in your heart that you cannot manage to say when you are sober.'

'Damn it, Patrick. Other men's valets will at least lie to them when they have made fools of themselves.'

'If it is any consolation, sir, Lord Endsted's valet often has cause to lie to his master on that score. We have discussed it.'

Tony held up a hand. 'Let us hear no more of Viscount Endsted. My night is quite grim enough, without thinking of him, or knowing that valets trade stories when they are gathered together. It chills the blood. Instead, tell me, Patrick, since you are so full of honesty, what am I to do to make amends with the Duchess of Wellford?'

'Perhaps, sir, it would go a long way to restoring her good humour, if you did the thing that she wished you to do in the first place.'

'You have returned early, your Grace.' Susan was looking at her with curiosity, no doubt trying to spy some evidence of carnal activity. 'Was the gentleman you wished to visit not at home?'

'On the contrary, he was in, and willing to see me.'

'That was quick.' Susan's face moued in disapproval. 'But I suppose it's the same with all men. The more time we takes on our appearance, the less time they needs. It don't seem right, somehow.'

Constance started at the familiarity, then admitted the truth. 'He sent me home. He took one good look at me, and he sent me away.' She looked at her maid, hoping that Susan could provide some explanation.

'He did not find you attractive?'

She sat on the end of the bed, shivering in the damp gown. 'He as much as said he did. He made comment on my appearance. He knew how I expected the evening to end. And he turned me down. I fear I have insulted him. Or lessened his opinion of me.'

'Then your friend left you to settle with Lord Barton yourself?' Susan looked more than a little dismayed at the thought.

'No. There was no problem about that. Mr Smythe said he was most willing to help, but that my gratitude was not necessary. Then he covered me up and sent me away.'

Susan sat on the end of the bed as well, clearly baffled. 'Forgive me for saying it, your Grace, but he must be a most unusual gentleman.'

Constance frowned. 'I think so as well, Susan.'

Anthony stared at the locked door of Barton's safe, and felt the sweat forming on his palms. He wiped his hands on his trouser legs and removed the picks from his coat pocket. Now was not the time for a display of weak nerves or a distaste for the work at hand. He could fulfil his promise to Stanton and destroy the plates by burning the house down if he could not manage to open the safe.

But for the promise to Constance? A fire would do him no good, for it would destroy the thing he searched for. And she wanted immediate action.

Patrick had been right. It had been stupid of him to give way to temper, and waste the better part of the evening with drink. When reason had begun to return, he had realised that he might need every spare moment between now and Monday, working on the lock, if he wished to deliver the deed to Constance and forestall Barton. He had been forced to spend several more hours becoming sober enough to do the job at all, and still might not be unaffected enough to do it well.

Now, it was past three and he had but a few hours before dawn. It was the quietest part of the night, when all good men were asleep, leaving the bad ones the freedom to work in peace.

Entry to the study was as uneventful as it had been the night of Barton's ball, even though he'd climbed up a drainpipe and into the window instead of using the stairs. Would that the results with the safe would be more successful than the last attempt.

The thing was still there, taunting him from its place on the wall behind the desk. Barton had not even bothered to conceal it, leaving its obvious presence as a sign of its impregnability.

If the man had anything of value, it was most assuredly behind the locked safe door. Tony had found the printing press in the basement along with the rest of the supplies, hidden under a Holland cloth, with little effort made to conceal them.

But there was no law against owning a press. To rid Barton of the paper would require one lucifer and the work of a moment, perhaps doused with the ink. Tony did not know if ink was particularly flammable, but, since so many things were, it was quite possible.

The engraved plates had to be somewhere in the house or the press would be useless. He fitted his pick into the lock and felt for the sliders, working one, and then another before feeling the pick slip. And now he must start over.

How many were there supposed to be? As many as eighteen, and any mistake meant a new beginning and more time wasted. He tried again, progressed slightly further and felt the pick slip in his sweaty hands.

Damn it. Damn it all to hell. He swore silently and repeatedly. Then he took a deep breath and began again.

It would have to work, because he would not return to Constance empty handed. He imagined her as she had been when she visited him. Huge, dark eyes, smooth skin, red lips, body soft and willing.

And he had sent her away. He must have been mad.

Of course, what was one night of gratitude against a lifetime of devotion, if there was some way she could be persuaded to see his intentions towards her ran deeper than the physical? In the end, she would think him no better than Barton, if he took advantage of her need. There would be time, later, if he could wait.

He felt his pick catch another slider and move it into position. And he focused on the touch of the lock and the vision in his mind of her leaning close to whisper softly in his ear.

There was a click of the room's door handle, which seemed as loud as a rifle shot in the dead silence of the house. Tony withdrew his pick and darted behind a curtain, praying that the velvet was not swaying to mark the passage of his body.

He could see the light at the edge of the curtain; the glow was faint, as though someone had entered the room, bearing a single candle.

A man, by the stride. Long, and with the click of a boot heel.

Barton.

Pace, pace, pace. Tony counted out enough steps for a man of nearly six foot to reach the desk.

He held his breath.

There was a faint rattle as a drawer was unlocked. The rustle of paper. A pause. A sigh. The sound of retreating footsteps, along with the retreating light. And the click of a door latch again.

Tony grinned to himself. Where best to keep a deed? In a safe? Hardly necessary, since no one would be seeking it. Best to keep it close, where one could admire it. Touch it when one wanted to reassure oneself of victory and fantasise over the conquered in the dark of night.

All in all, he was lucky that Barton was not keeping the document at his bedside. Perhaps with the prospect of Constance so firmly in his grasp, the deed was not necessary.

Tony stepped from behind the curtain and produced a penknife, then slid it along the space in the desk drawer until he heard a satisfying click. He opened the drawer and found the deed, face up in plain view.

Too easy, really, once one left common sense behind and entered the realm of obsession. He could almost feel sorry for Barton, had the man chosen a different object for his passion.

Tony folded the paper and tucked it into a pocket. He went to the window and was gone.

Chapter Nine

Music played softly in the background and Constance sipped her champagne and pretended to enjoy herself. Sunday night's ball at the townhouse of the Earl of Stanton was to have been a night of pure pleasure in the company of friends. She had been looking forward to it for weeks. And now Barton had ruined everything. The music made no impact and the drink held no flavour. All she could think about was the impending doom of Monday morning and the cold look on Tony's face as he had sent her away.

Her friend, the countess, had hugged her when she had seen the expression on Constance's face, and enquired after her health.

She had pretended that nothing was wrong, but even the earl had noticed the change in her and remarked on it. And Esme had clasped her hand again and assured her that, whatever the problem might be, she had but to ask, and they would find a way to resolve it. She could treat the Stanton home as her own, if need be. Stay the night or longer, if she wished. And take pleasure in the entertainment at hand, for it was expected to be most fine.

Constance had insisted that she was in no dire need, and that her friend needn't worry, although the earl's look at her as she passed through the receiving line was too shrewd and it was clear that he was not fooled.

It had been a mistake to lie at all. For it would look even worse to her hosts when she needed to swallow her pride and beg Esme for refuge at the end of the evening, if it was to be a choice between her house and her honour.

There was some comfort, at least, in knowing that only the best company was invited through these particular doors. She had no reason to fear a run in with Barton before the morning, for such as he would never gain entrance to a ball held by the Stantons.

Which made it all the more surprising to see Anthony Smythe in close conversation with the host. The earl could not possibly know the man's true occupation, or St John would throw him bodily from the room. And Constance could not very well inform them of what she knew. Certainly not when she had gone to Mr Smythe, requesting the very service she pretended to abhor.

He was across the room from her, and she tried to resist the urge to look in his direction. How utterly mortifying it had been to go to him, practically bare and obviously willing, only to be patted on the head and put from the room. If she had behaved in a similar manner, with any of the other men of her acquaintance…

Then she need not have gone to Mr Smythe at all. Upon seeing how she had costumed herself, and hearing of her willingness to co-operate, they'd have given her any sum she required to clear her debts. The ink would scarcely be dry on the cheque before they'd have taken her up on her offer.

Then why, for the sake of her already-battered spirit, had she gone to the only man unwilling to take her body as payment? Was it because she had known in her heart that he would be too honourable to accept?

Or simply because she wanted a reason, any reason at all, to see him again, tempt him in a way that would make him forget her behaviour in the library, and offer him no resistance when he pulled her close, laid her down, and took from her what she wanted to give him?

It had been so easy to restrain herself through the last year, as the suggestions she'd received had become bolder and bolder. And, on some level, she'd known that if there was no one to offer her marriage, there might be one whose offer was not quite so insulting as the rest. She had no desire to be a mistress. That would be no better than marrying for money.

But if there were a man who valued her, and whose company she enjoyed, and if he was willing to be discreet? She would gladly yield just to feel arms around her again, and lips on her temple, and to sleep secure in the knowledge that someone cared about her, even if it was for only a night.

She glanced into a mirror at the far end of the room, catching a glimpse of the image of Tony Smythe reflected back to her. His dark blue coat fit smoothly over the muscles she felt when he'd held her. His legs, as well, were straight and strong from climbing, and graceful as he walked. She thought she could hear his distant laugh, and could imagine the light in his eyes, and the way his smile curved a little higher on one side than the other.

It was a face not so much beautiful as it was interesting. There was energy in it, and enthusiasm. One could look at it for a lifetime and always see something different. And when he had a passion for something, or someone, his excitement would be impossible to resist.

Constance averted her gaze from the mirror, casting her eyes downward, focusing on the trails of bubbles arising from her champagne. It did no good to watch him now. She might see the one thing she most feared, a look of pity in the eyes for her pathetic behaviour of the night before, and confirmation of his lack of success in getting the thing she needed. How had she expected him to manage in a night what might take days of planning? She was a fool to even ask him.

And she would look an even bigger fool, if he caught her spying on him in public.

'Would you stand up with me, your Grace?'

She was startled. He was close to her now, standing beside her, and she'd never heard him approach. Her heart was pounding in response to his nearness, and it was not because of fright.

He gestured to the dance floor. There was polite interest on his face now. Neither more nor less than she would expect from any of the other men attending.

'I would be delighted, Mr Smythe.' She tried to read his face, but it gave no clue. Did he have news for her? She was dying to ask it, but what was the point in swearing him to secrecy if she blurted out the whole truth in a crowded ballroom?

They took their place in the set and he bowed to her, and the music began.

He was an excellent dancer. His steps were sure and his touch light as he guided her down the row. She tried to relax and enjoy herself, but his steady gaze was both pleasant and unnerving. He wanted to tell her something, she was sure.

And found herself wishing that that was not the reason for the intensity when he looked at her. Robert had not cared much for dancing, and was most relieved when other men had been willing to stand up with her in his place. But none of them would dare gaze at her so, with the duke in the room.

She had watched other young ladies, and watched their beaus watching them. She had thought it sweet and tried not to lament on it. Men had looked at her thus once, very long ago, but so long ago that she could hardly remember how it felt.

They had looked as Anthony Smythe was looking at her now. His hand took hers again and he smiled. When it was their turn to wait at the bottom of the set, he leaned closer to her, and said, 'You are very lovely tonight.'

'Thank you.' She wondered if that was the case.

He must have seen the doubt in her eyes. 'You were lovely last night, as well.'

'You did not seem to think it at the time.'

'On the contrary. You were inordinately tempting. But speed was of the essence, was it not? If I had accepted your offer, we would be there still, on the floor of my parlour, too exhausted to move.'

She stared around her, to make sure no one had heard him speak. And, as always, he had taken care that the other guests would know nothing of his scandalous comments, but her delighted blush might make them stare.

'I am just as diligent and careful in taking pleasure as I am in doing business, and I take care not to mix the two. In the future, there will be ample time to spend together, if you still wish it. But if I had lost myself in you last night, I would have quite forgotten to go to Barton and get the thing that you wished me to retrieve.'

She opened her mouth to speak, and he smiled placidly.

'Please act as though nothing has happened. Remember where we are, your Grace.'

He was right. Throwing her arms around his neck and begging to see it this instant was sure to incite comment. But she could not help the joy that showed upon her face.

He looked at her, smiled back and said, 'The look on your face right now is payment enough for me. Have you forgiven me for last night?'

'There is nothing to forgive. It was I—'

'Shh. Let us hear none of that. May I visit you, later? With your permission, I will come to your house, to return the thing that concerned you so.'

She whispered, 'I shall leave here immediately and tell my servants to expect you.'

'You shall do nothing of the kind. No one need know of what has transpired between us. Enjoy your time here, for Esme is a particular friend of yours, is she not? And this is a delightful ball. It would be a shame to go so soon. Return home after midnight, send your maid to bed and wait for me at one.'

She nodded, wondering how he knew of her friendships, for she had not told him.

And he nodded back to acknowledge her assent and led her through the rest of the dance as though nothing unusual had happened, with an occasional comment about the music, the fine quality of the food, and the fact that summer had been uncommonly warm.

But he continued to fix her with the same intense gaze that had unsettled her before.

He was coming to her rooms later, and in secret. She found the prospect quite exciting. And with the way he was looking at her, perhaps he had decided to mix business and pleasure after all. It was not so surprising, she reminded herself. Despite what they might claim to put one off one's guard, men had needs and would act on them, given the opportunity.

He might say that he was honoured to help and needed no reward, but he had taken great risk to do what she had asked. She doubted that he would deny her or himself, once they were alone. And try as she might, she could not bring herself to be bothered. Why, if Lord Barton's offer had been so distasteful to her, was she not offended now?

Because she did not want to lie with Barton, as she did with Anthony Smythe.

The thought of them together warmed her blood. She wanted to feel his hands upon her and see that crooked smile in the firelight as he took her. Her stomach gave a lurch at the thought and her steps faltered.

And he caught her hand and led her on, smiling in curiosity at the look that must be on her face, but making no comment.

Very well, then. Her virtue was not as steadfast as she had once thought. And she did miss the touch of a man, just as everyone kept reminding her.

Everyone except Tony.

Perhaps that was why she wanted him so.

The dance ended and she moved through the rest of the evening as if on a cloud. Her home was safe. Barton had no hold on her. And when she retired, she would have Tony.

When Esme saw her again, as she said her goodbyes, she proclaimed her looking better. The food and the dancing must have done her good, for she was in fine colour. Almost blushing.

Constance smiled the secret back to herself and agreed that she was feeling worlds better, and that she intended to retire early. Then she returned home, prepared for bed and sent the maid away. The lawn of her nightdress was crisp and cool against her fevered skin as she unlatched the window and waited for the clock to strike one.

As the bell was chiming, he stepped over the sill, smiling back at the window she had left open for him. 'Thank you for the small courtesy, your Grace. It is rare to enter in this way and find evidence that I am welcome. Most refreshing.'

'Did you find the deed?' She hurried to his side.

'What? No "Hello, Tony. So good to see you.

Lovely dancing this evening..." No preamble. Small talk? Chit-chat?' He grinned. 'I supposed not.' He reached into his pocket and brought out a document, which he laid upon her night table. 'It is exactly as you said. In your husband's hand, the house is deeded to you. And here is the attached inventory. Put it somewhere safe. Your bank, perhaps. But do not trust it to that young jackanapes that holds your husband's title. And do not mention it to Barton until you have to. He will know that someone has got into his study and taken it, and you do not want to be associated with other thefts that might occur there. I will be visiting him again, before my business with him is done, and he will be on guard against me.

'If you can just stall him for a time, he will forget his plans for you, for I dare say he will have troubles enough soon and little time to pursue you.'

She wondered if this might have something to do with the theft at the ball, but was afraid to ask. Instead she looked down at the deed, which need be her only concern. She swallowed. 'It is such a relief to know that, no matter what, the house is mine.'

Then she looked at him significantly. 'And I am so very grateful. How can I ever repay you?' And she leaned close to him in the moonlight and waited for the obvious suggestion.

He smiled. 'No thanks are necessary. It is enough to know that I have helped a woman in distress.'

'No thanks. At all.' She hoped her disappointment was not too plain.

'I know something of hardship, and of being forced to make decisions that might compromise myself, for the sake of stability. I would not wish it on another.'

'Many men would take advantage, given the circumstances. You held the deed yourself and could just has easily have used it against me.'

'But I would not.'

'I am sorry to create more work for you, when I can do nothing in return for you.'

He sighed. 'Some day, quite without even thinking, you might do a thing that seems like a trifle to you, but will make all my efforts on your part seem as nothing. Until then, do not trouble yourself. While it would be easy to accept what you are trying to give me, I fear you might live to regret it. If I succumb, in the end you will think me no better than Barton. You are safe now, but if Barton, or any other, should prove difficult, please feel free to call upon me.' He started towards the window.

She followed him, searching for something that might stay him a little longer. 'Will I see you again?'

He smiled. 'It is likely. You have seen me many times before, you know. I certainly knew of you. But we have not been introduced until just recently. Now you know me, I suspect you will not be able to help but run into me again.'

'I should like that.' She touched his sleeve.

He had reached the window and then turned back when he felt her touch. 'I should like that as well. Under better circumstances.' He put his hand on the sill, ready to lift himself over the edge.

And she remembered the first night, when he had assured her of his character, and hazarded a bolt. 'Your wife is very fortunate to have such an honest thief for a husband.'

He pushed away from the sill and turned back to her. 'Wife?' He looked puzzled. 'I have none.'

'But when we first met—'

'When I was robbing your jewel case,' he reminded her.

'You said that you had loved but once, and I thought perhaps...'

He shook his head and stepped back into the room. He opened his mouth to speak, closed it again, and paused to take a deep breath. Then he said, 'And this is where I admit the truth, and you think me a fool. I've loved but once. But she has never loved me. It has been years... We were childhood friends.' He shook his head again and muttered, 'That puts too fine a gloss on it.' And then he admitted, 'We were acquaintances. I was too terrified to speak to her.'

'You, afraid to speak to a woman?' She stared at him incredulously.

He looked into her eyes and nodded. 'I was then. And I still am, when it comes to her.'

'Because she rejected you, all those years ago.'

He shook his head. 'She did not give that much thought to me, I'm afraid. I doubt she said three words to me in the time we knew each other. She married young and well.' He looked up at her. 'She is as high above me as you are. And as beautiful. But I doubt she would know me if we passed in the street. She has forgotten all about me. There can never be anything between us, of course. How can there be, if but one of us loves?'

She took a step towards him. 'But that is so sad. And you have kept yourself for her, all these years?'

'Not as such. I have known the company of women, of course. But my heart is elsewhere. I do not wish to marry, if I cannot have her.'

'But if you do not marry, you will not have children.' The next question mocked her, but she forced herself to ask it. 'Do you not wish for a son?'

He looked genuinely puzzled. 'I had not honestly given it much thought.'

'You did not think on it?' It was her turn to look puzzled. So many hours of her life and her husband's had been consumed with the subject of children. And here was a man who did not think about it at all. 'But you will have no heir.'

'Of course I will have an heir. I am quite well stocked with nephews. I have two of them, and a niece as well. I have been "dear Uncle Tony" for so long I can hardly remember a time when I wasn't. And I have done my share to raise them up. I always assumed that what was mine now would some day be theirs.' He smiled fondly, as he thought of children that had been fathered by others.

'But they are not *yours*,' she insisted.

'As much mine as anyone's. Their fathers are long dead. They have stepfathers now, at last. So the burden is no longer solely mine.'

'You do not care for children,' she surmised.

He shook his head. 'You misunderstand. The raising of them was not so much of a burden, even at its worst. I like children. And I would welcome my own, should any appear through design or carelessness. But it has always seemed to me to be a frivolous thing to insist on raising the fruit of one's loins when one is surrounded by windfalls.'

He would not care, even if he has already guessed the truth. Her legs almost collapsed under her, her knees trembled so. 'Then, if your wife could not give you children?'

'If the wife of my choosing could not give me children?' He sighed. 'If I could but get her to give herself to me, it would be more than I ever expected. What kind of fool would I be to win my heart's desire and then find fault with her for a thing that was not under our control?'

What kind of fool would he be? A fool like her husband and all the other men of her acquaintance. Children did not matter to Tony. If he wanted her, he would have her, and not think twice about her infertility. There would be no snide offer of fun and games, followed by a pitying smile when the talk came to marriage.

'It would not matter to me in the slightest. There is but one woman for me, Constance. And I will not love another, as long as there is life left in us, and even the smallest chance.' He looked into her eyes and it was as if he were looking into her very soul and making the vow to her.

He shook his head again and looked down, unable to meet her gaze. 'I do not expect you to understand. It really sounds quite mad, when I explain it thus.'

'Oh, no. I understand perfectly.' And, suddenly, she did. It was possible to fall hopelessly in love with someone who was totally wrong for you, and even worse, could never love you back, because of a foolish fantasy of perfection that he'd been carrying with him for his entire life. How could one compete with that?

He was smiling at her again. 'That is most kind of you to say so. Because…' He appeared to be about to speak. But he said nothing. There was a pause that seemed ready to become long and awkward.

So there was nothing wrong with her. He did not wish to raise false hopes by a casual seduction that would lead nowhere. He respected her. She should feel more relief than frustration. She broke the silence. 'Do not feel you need to explain yourself further. I think it is very noble of you. I have often wondered what it might be like to be as brave as you and to not care for reputation or stability, hazarding all for the sake of love. But I fear I am disappointingly practical, far too concerned with my own security in the distant future to risk following my heart on the moment. Still, I very much enjoy seeing others do so, and will pray fervently for your good fortune. I fear some of us are not destined to feel that kind of grand passion.'

If possible, he looked even more mortified than he had the night she came to him to ask for the deed. He coloured again, and his eyes fell. And when he looked up, his expression was earnest, as it had been when she had seen him in the library. 'Do not say that. Do not ever say that. You deserve all that love can give, and you should settle for nothing else.' And when he pulled her to him, it was shockingly sudden and she had just enough time to lift her face to his kiss.

It wasn't the same kiss that he had taken from her on the night they met. This one was hard and demanding. A soul-deep kiss, full of desire. And she kissed him back, hoping that the night might last just a little longer, that he might forget himself and stay.

He devoured her mouth and she took his tongue, thrusting into his mouth in return. And she felt his hand opening the buttons on her nightdress, cupping a breast and pinching the nipple between his fingers until she moaned.

She pushed her leg between his, and rocked her body against him. There was no question that he wanted her as she wanted him and she reached to pull him even closer so that he might know how well their bodies would fit together.

He pulled away from her, then, shaking his head. And he said, 'I must go.' He laughed, and it was unsteady. 'Although you do make it most difficult to leave. Especially since I need my body to obey me as I climb down from your window, and it is making it almost painfully clear to me that it would much rather stay here with you.'

But his eyes were bright with excitement as he said, 'I promise you, soon. But alas, I must not stay tonight. I have other work I must do before the sun rises. I cannot spend it in play with you. Besides, I have no desire to rush what I will do with you, the next time we are alone.' He traced the line of her throat downwards with his finger to massage her breast again. 'Are we in agreement?'

She nodded, dazed at the idea.

'Very good, then.' She looked into his eyes, and her body trembled at the suggestions in them. 'And remember, if you need anything at all before I come to you again, you know my direction. Feel free to call on me, or send a message and I will come to you. But do not think that you ever need walk through life alone, or that you must be practical instead of happy.'

And he was gone again, taking her heart with him.

'What do you mean, you did not tell her?'

Tony stared down into the glass in his hand, and willed himself not to throw it. But with Patrick standing between him and the fire, the temptation presented itself.

'I mean,' he responded to his valet, 'that it is a damned tricky thing, when you have been speaking to a woman as one person, to suddenly come out and admit that you are not who you seem to be. I thought, once Barton was gotten out of the way, and there was nothing standing between us, it would be easier.

'And in a way it was. She was not the false jade she played in my sitting room last night. She was much more herself, grateful, but not brazen. She cared enough to make conversation. She asked about me. She made it plain that she wanted to know me better.'

He remembered the feel of her body against his and her breast in his hand. 'She was willing to know me even better, by the end, I dare say. And I did declare my continued and unwavering devotion.' He shrugged. 'Not technically to her, but I believe she was responding well, even though I did not specifically say I was speaking of her.

'But then she declared me too noble and showed

signs of giving me up entirely, for my own good, so that I could continue to worship her from afar. And so I kissed her again, and then everything got fuzzy and I quite forgot how it was I meant to go on. But I had to get back to Stanton's damn ball since he wanted to speak to me in private, after. I could not very well drop anchor for the night.' He grinned. 'Although I got the distinct impression, there at the last, that I would have been a welcome guest, had I decided to do so.'

Patrick smacked his forehead with the palm of his hand. 'But now she has the deed, and you have no reason to see her again.'

'On the contrary, I have every reason. She might pretend uninterest during the day, but she has kissed me again. That is the third time and it is not often enough.

'Now that she has noticed me, I plan to be very much under foot. She cannot ignore me for ever. Perhaps next time we meet, I will not need to climb through her bedroom window. If I am not conversing with her in her bedroom, it will be much easier to keep my head.'

And perhaps, in good light, she will recognise me. He did not want to think it. He did not want it to matter. And yet, it mattered so very much.

Patrick replied with confidence, 'Once you tell her the truth, there will be no problem at all.'

Other than accepting that, if I am not attempting to

rob her, I am utterly forgettable. 'It is rather embarrassing, not to have told her from the first.' He tried to toss the comment out in a way that made it unimportant.

'It will only grow more embarrassing as time passes.' Damn Patrick and his reasonable advice.

'I gathered that. But it is vexing to have my true nature go unrecognised by one who has known me my whole life.' There. The truth would out, somewhere, if not where he needed it.

'Your true nature?' Patrick snorted. 'And by true nature, you mean the nice young cleric who pulled me out of Newgate, pretending charity, but really wanting me to help him dispose of his ill-gotten gains?'

Tony bristled. 'That is most unfair.'

'But it is the truth. You were only too happy to learn all I could teach you, and assume all the risks, while sensible men such as myself preferred to retire from crime and devote themselves to pressing milord's coat and perfecting the knot for a Mathematical cravat.'

Patrick was staring at him in disbelief. 'You insist on seeing yourself as no different than you were when you were children. But you are both changed by the past thirteen years. Your true nature, as you put it, was not in evidence when she saw you last. She paid you no heed then because there was no reason to. You were shy, bookish and painfully honest. It was easy enough to cure you of the honesty, and now that you are putting your education to use, you are not so quiet as you once were. Once you rid yourself of the shyness, there will be nothing left at all of the old you, not even the name. And you have her complete attention, do you not? She does not love another?'

'There is Endsted,' Tony admitted.

Patrick snorted. 'Then you have nothing to fear. The results are guaranteed, once you declare yourself to her.'

Perhaps Patrick was right. 'Very well, then. I shall call on her tomorrow. At her home this time, so she has no reason to be distracted by a rival. I have no doubt she will welcome me, since she said as much last night. In daylight with the servants about and a respectable distance between us, it will be much easier to part with the truth. And then we shall see how things go.' And he knew the path was right because of the sudden flare of hope that sprang beside the banked fires of desire in his heart.

Chapter Ten

The next morning, Constance paced her rooms, uneasily, looking at the deed on the night table. And the note beside it: *We must talk. Barton.*

The note had arrived with the morning's post, even before she could get the deed to the bank. And now she was afraid to leave the house with it, lest he be waiting outside to take it from her again. He knew. That had to be the truth of it. If he thought he was still in possession of the deed, he would have marched boldly into the house this morning, as he had threatened to do. Instead, he had missed the thing, and guessed her involvement in the theft. He meant to harass her about it. Perhaps he would go to the Runners.

But what could he do? He could not very well claim the deed was his and she had taken it, since it clearly stated that she was the owner of the house. Tony was right. She had but to avoid him, until he lost interest, and her life would return to normal and the already-long string of problems that she must deal with. But the sale of the house, along with the last of Mr Smythe's purse, would lend some time in which she could think.

And what was she to do about Anthony Smythe? It was all so much more complicated in daylight than in moonlight. She wanted to see him again. As soon as possible. The pull on her heart was undeniable.

And he could help her against Barton. She pushed the note to the side, hiding it under her copy of *The Times*. Tony had helped her before, and proven a powerful ally. She needed help again. He was attracted to her, and knew she was attracted to him, but he showed no intention of forcing her to take action.

She knew what action she wished to take. But in the morning, she could remember why it was wrong of her to want him as she did.

She listed the reasons against it. She knew nothing of his family or his life. He was a criminal, albeit a charming one. And he loved elsewhere.

And on her side, if she took one lover, it would be easier to take a second, once the first lost interest. And then a third. And some day, she would awake to find she had no lover, no husband and no reputation. If she wished for marriage, she must not begin by settling for less.

Yet it was hard to think beyond the moment. She

could have his help and his affection, should she but ask. He might leave some day. But she remembered the feel of his hands upon her, and the rushing in her that was unlike anything she had ever felt for Robert. He might leave and she might find another. But who was to say that her next husband could arouse such passion in her? If she did not give in to him now, she might never know that feeling again.

Her teacup trembled in her hand. Very well, then. She would ask him to be careful of her reputation, but she would yield to him as soon as he asked. And no one need ever know of it, but the two of them.

And then she stared down at the front page of her paper. A hanging. She stared down at the article, reading with horrible fascination. The man had been a burglar, stealing purses from a rooming house. The gallows mechanism had failed, and his body had dropped scant inches, leaving him to dance out the last of his life for nearly an hour. And the whole time his wife and children had stood, at the foot of the gibbet, pleading for leniency, or at least a quick death. The crowd had not wanted their fun spoiled and had mocked them, laughing and pelting them with offal until they had run from the scene. And the woman had lacked even the money necessary to retrieve the body for burial.

She imagined the man, spasming out the last of his life in front of a cheering throng while his family stood by, helpless. And then she imagined Tony, dancing for the hangman, and standing below him, crying her heart out and unable to help.

But if she kept to her current plan, it would be even worse. Then, she would hide in her house, afraid for her precious reputation, leaving him to die alone and friendless. And she could read in *The Times*, the next day, how he had suffered for the amusement of the crowd. She would hate herself, to her last breath, knowing that the man she loved had suffered, and she had done nothing to help.

Her hand jerked as a shudder racked her, and the tea spilled on to the paper, blurring the words.

'Your Grace, there is a gentleman come to call.' Her maid was holding a salver.

'I am not at home to Lord Barton.'

'Not Barton, your Grace. Mr Smythe.' Susan had guessed the identity of her visitor, and was grinning in anticipation.

Constance stared in fascination at the card upon the tray. She wanted to go to the parlour, grab the man by the hand and pull him upstairs with her. If she asked him, he could help her forget Barton, Freddy and the horrible thing she had just read. For a few hours. And then she would have to come downstairs and face reality again. A tryst with Mr Smythe would be lovely while it lasted. But what future could there be in it?

Only the one she had just seen.

'I am not at home. Not to anyone. If you need me, I shall be in the garden, but whoever else may call, I am not at home.'

She tried not to rush as she took the back stairs, far away from where anyone at the front of the house might see or hear her. Stopping in the tiny still room by the kitchen, she found a bonnet and basket, and her pruning scissors. It would all be easier in the garden, surrounded by her flowers and herbs. The sights, the smells, the taste. Everything made more sense there.

She stepped out into the sunlight, feeling the protection of the high brick walls on all sides that muffled the sound of the city. Here, there was only birdsong, the faint trickle of a fountain, and the fragrances of the plants. She ran down the path that led to the wrought-iron gate and the street, to the small bench hidden in the shade of a tree.

She sank down upon it, and let the tears slide down her cheeks again, now that she was safe where no one could see her. Her shoulders shook with the effort of containing the sobs. She did not want to be alone any more, and there was a man willing and full of life who could take the loneliness away. It was so unfair, that the one thing she wanted could lead to a pain and loneliness greater than anything she had felt before.

It had been hard to watch Robert die, but he had been older, and they had known the time would come. But Tony was likely to die a young man, suddenly and violently. And despite it all, she wanted him beyond all reason, aching with it.

And she heard a sigh and a faint rattle of the gate. She looked up to see Smythe, hands wrapped around the bars of the gate, observing her.

She wiped her face dry on the back of her sleeve. 'Mr Smythe! What are you doing here?'

He was nonplussed to be discovered. 'I beg your pardon, your Grace. I…I…I did not mean to spy on you.'

The stutter surprised her. When he came to her at night, there was no hesitation, only resolute action. But now, he seemed almost shy when talking to her. He was a different person in daylight. But then, so was she, or she would have opened the door for him when he had come calling.

She tried a false smile, hoping it did not look too wet around the edges. 'You did not mean to spy, or you did not mean to be caught spying?'

He released the gate and held out open hands, and there was a flash of the smile she recognised. 'I did not expect to find you here. I was told that you were not at home.' There was the barest hint of censure there.

'And yet you came to the back of my house. Were you looking for something?'

He leaned his forehead against the iron of the gate. 'I often walk by on this street. And you must admit, the view of the garden is most restful. I greatly admire it.' He stared wistfully in at her.

She gave up. At least, if he were near, she could touch him and reassure herself that the fancy she'd been spinning was not yet reality. She rose. 'You might as well come in, then, and have a better look.'

Without further invitation, he took a few steps back, and ran at the gate, catching a bar easily and swinging his body over the spikes at the top with inches to spare, landing on his feet on the other side.

There was an awkward pause.

'I meant to open that for you, you know.' She hoped the reproof in her voice hid the thrill of excitement that she felt in watching him move. He was still very much alive, and it did her heart good to see it. She sat back down, arranging her skirts to hide her confusion.

'I am sorry. It was most foolish of me. I am sometimes moved to rash actions. Rather like spying on you in your garden a moment ago, and then lying about my fondness of flowers to gain entrance.'

There was another awkward pause.

'Not that I am not fond of flowers,' he amended. 'And yours are most charmingly arranged.'

'Thank you.' She patted the seat on the bench beside her, and he came towards her. His stride had the same easy grace she saw in the ballroom and in the bedroom, and she tried not to appear too observant of it. 'Do you know much of flowers?'

He smiled. 'Not a thing. I can recognise a rose, of course. I'm not a total idiot. But I tend to take most notice of the plants that provide cover when I am gaining entrance to a house.' He touched the bush he was standing beside.

'Rosemary,' she prompted.

'Eh?'

'The shrub you are touching is rosemary.'

He plucked a sprig and crushed it between his fingers, and the air around them was full of the scent. 'For remembrance.' He held it out to her.

'You know your Shakespeare.'

'If you knew me, you would find me surprisingly well read.'

'Is that important? In your line of work, I mean.'

He dropped the rosemary and looked away. 'I am more than my work, you know.'

'I didn't mean to imply…'

His eyes were sad when he looked back to her. 'There was a time when I intended something other than the life I chose. I was the third son, and there was not very much money. I knew that there would be even less, once I was of age and my brothers had families to support. I would need to fend for myself.'

She felt a rush of sympathy. He had been lonely, even in a large family.

He continued. 'What I wanted did not matter, in any case. My oldest brother was killed duelling, and the second took a bullet to the brain at Talavera. And suddenly, there was only me, two widows, two nephews and a niece. My brothers were older, but not necessarily wiser. Their estates were in shambles and they had made no provisions for their deaths. The whole family was bound for the poorhouse, unless I took drastic action.' He shrugged. 'There are many who have more than they need.'

'But surely, an honest profession. You could have read for divinity.' She looked at his politely incredulous expression and tried to imagine him a vicar. 'Perhaps not.'

He sat down at her side. 'It was my plan, once. And I went to interview for a living, hoping that I would be able to send some small monies home. But the lord met me at a public house to tell me that it had gone to another.

'And when he got up to leave, he forgot his purse. I was halfway out the door to return it, when it occurred to me that he had money enough to fill many such purses, and my family had no food on the table and no prospects for the future. I put the purse in my pocket, and brought the money home to my family. And that was the end of that.' He smiled, obviously happier thinking of theft than he had been thinking of life as a clergyman. 'And what of you? Did you always plan on the life you got?'

She frowned. 'Yes. I suppose I did. My mother raised me so that I might be an asset to any man that might offer for me. And she encouraged me, when offers were made, to choose carefully in return so that I might never want. Until Robert died, things had gone very much as I would have hoped. I would have liked children, of course.'

'It is not too late,' Smythe responded.

She resisted the urge to explain matters to him plainly. 'I fear it is not on the cards for me. But beside that one small thing, my life was everything I might have hoped for. I made a most advantageous marriage.'

'You were happy, then?'

She answered as if by rote, 'I had money, social position and a husband who treated me well. I had no right to complain.'

'That did not answer the question.'

'Of course I was happy,' she said in frustration.

'And yet, when you say it thus, I wonder if you were.'

She sighed. 'It is different for men than for women. If you have a talent for something, you can proceed in a way that will develop it and find a career that will make the best use of your abilities. There are options open. You might study law, or go into the military, or become a vicar.'

'Or a thief,' he reminded her.

She nodded. 'But because I was born female, it was my fate to marry. It is not as if I could expect another future. Fortunately, I had no talent to speak of, or any other natural ability than to be beautiful, or I might have felt some disappointment about that fact.'

He looked at her in surprise. 'No natural talent? I'll

grant you, you are a beauty, a nonpareil. But you are wrong to think you have no other virtues. You are intelligent, well read, and you have a sharp and agile wit.'

She laughed. 'You base these fine compliments on an acquaintance of several days. My dear Mr Smythe, I would be a fool to be flattered by one with such a shallow understanding of me. There was nothing about my character, my wealth or my family that would have led Robert to want me, had I not been a beauty. I assure you, it was a great weight off my parents to know, before they died, that I was to be well taken care of.'

Tony shook his head. 'That sounds as if you were a burden to your family. But your parents spoke often of your fine character, although your mother was most proud of her only child being so well placed.'

She glanced at him sharply. 'You speak as if you knew her.'

'We were acquainted,' he replied. 'I knew your father, as well. I sympathise with your loss of them.'

'You knew them both?' She started. 'They never mentioned you.'

'It was a long time ago. You had been gone from the house for several years when last I met them. And they never knew of this.' He made a vague gesture, meant to encompass his life. 'Believe me, I never visited them in my professional capacity.'

'I never suspected that you would.' And it was strange, but she trusted his word on the matter.

'You are being unfair to yourself, if you think you are without talent, or suspect that you might have no value to a husband other than to beautify his home.'

But the one thing that Robert had most wanted from her, she had been unable to give him, and she held her tongue.

'I know for a fact that you are much more intelligent than you appear, even if you pretend it is not so in the presence of the Endsteds of the world. I saw the books he was carrying for you, and the ones you keep in your room. Philosophy, Latin, French. Not the reading of a simple mind.'

'It is a pity, then, that I could not have put all that learning to use, and saved myself from the financial predicament I find myself in.'

He gazed at her with surprising intensity. 'You have managed most cleverly with little money or help, where a foolish woman could not have gone on at all. It is not your fault that you put your trust in people who should have protected you, only to have them fail you.'

She found his comments both flattering and embarrassing, and sought to turn the conversation back to familiar ground. She summoned her most flirtatious look, fixed him with it and said, 'How strange you are to say so. Most men content themselves, when I am alone with them, to comment on the fineness of my skin or the softness of my hand.'

He was having none of it, and responded matter of

factly, 'You know as well as I do the quality of your complexion. But I will comment on it, if you insist. Your skin is almost luminous in its clarity. Chinese porcelain cannot compare. But I also know that the skin is nothing to the brightness of the spirit it contains. I know you, your Grace, although you do not believe it. I do.'

She smiled, overwhelmed by his obvious sincerity. 'And I do not really know you at all.'

'You know my greatest secret: that I am a thief. It was embarrassing to be caught. But I was glad, when it happened, to find myself in the hands of such a charming captor.'

She blushed at the notion that she had taken him prisoner, and not the other way around. 'You really shouldn't steal, you know. It is wrong.'

'I am familiar with the commandments,' he said with asperity. 'And follow nine out of ten to the best of my ability. It is a better average, I think, than the people I steal from, who have no thought to any but themselves. They are greedy, indolent and licentious.'

'Is that why you came to my rooms? To punish me for my sins? Because I am guilty.' She hung her head. 'Of pride, and of lust.'

'Serious, of course, but the seven deadly sins are not in the Bible, *per se*,' he remarked. 'But what makes you think you are guilty of them?'

'Barton has been able to manipulate me easily, because he knows how carefully I guard my reputation. If I were willing to admit that I am poor, and that he has gulled me...'

'Then you might ruin any chance to marry well. You are not guilty of anything, other than being forced to place your trust in one who proved unworthy. Why should you suffer, while the Bartons of the world live in comfort? You could don a cap and remain a poor widow, I suppose. Take in sewing. Do good works. Live off the charity of the church, since your wastrel nephew cannot be bothered to live up to his obligations to you.' He made a face. 'It does not sound very pleasant. And it would be a waste of one as young and lovely as yourself, if there is any other alternative.'

He paused, and then added as an afterthought, 'You could marry below your station. No one would think you proud, then.'

'I will consider it, if someone asks. But none has. No one offers marriage at all. Men below my station avoid me as unattainable. And men who would be fine catches want nothing more than...' She shook her head. 'Barton says that he, and the others, can see that I secretly desire what they offer. That I am too willing, too interested in their company. That I allow too many small liberties, and they are surprised when I refuse to follow through.'

Smythe sniffed. 'Men have ever used this, when

trying to persuade a woman to do more than she wishes. It is no reflection on you. Ignore them.'

'But look how I behave, when I am alone with you.' She blurted the words and stopped, embarrassed to have told him the truth. 'I...I am wanton.'

He was grinning again. 'Yes. I noticed. It is most flattering. Tell me, is this how you behave with all the other men of your acquaintance?'

'Of course not. How dare you even think—?'

He laid a finger on her lips to silence her. 'I did not think so. But it is even more flattering to hear you admit that I am the only one to move you so.' He looked down at his feet, and she thought for a moment that she could see a faint blush in his cheek. Then he said, 'It is not so bad a thing, to take pleasure in the company of the opposite gender. Of course, I am biased, since I am the man in question. I would have to be made of stone to wish you less willing when in my embrace. And I would have been most put out to find you sighing over Barton's embrace, and behaving thus with him. But I would not expect that, just because you have lain with one man, that you are game to lie with any that might ask.

'And because you allow me a degree of intimacy, for which I am most grateful...' he looked up and smiled at her and there was a wicked glint in his eye that made her heart beat faster '...I do not assume that I can do as I please with you. If ever I make a suggestion that offends you, you have but to tell me to stop. I am yours to command.'

And thoughts appeared of what she wished to command him to do. They had nothing to do with stopping his current behaviour or being any less wicked in her presence. Quite the contrary. She blushed. 'No. It is quite all right. You have done nothing to offend me. I am…' She whispered the next words, 'I fear I am enjoying it too much.'

He whispered back to her. 'You have nothing to fear. As I told you the first night, your secrets are safe with me. All of your secrets. But if you enjoy my company so much, why were you not at home, when I called?'

'What we spoke of last night… I do not know if I can go through with it. It seemed so right, at the time. But it is foolish of me to make promises in the moonlight that I am afraid to keep in daylight.'

'I see.' He reached out and gently touched her arm. 'And why were you crying? This is the second time that I have come upon you and found you in tears. I do not believe you gave me a clear indication of the problem on that night, either. What is it that distresses you so?'

'I thought I informed you then that it was none of your concern.'

'But we hardly knew each other, then. I dare say we are much closer now. One might say, thick as thieves.' He considered. 'Although for the most part, I have not found thieves to be much in each other's confidence.'

'Then why should I trust you?'

'Because I care enough to ask, and sincerely hope that the problem will be something I can aid you in. You must admit, I have helped you before.'

She laughed through her tears. 'It is not so easy, this time, I fear. You tempt me. And it is hard to resist you. But the gentleman you discovered me with in the library? I had hopes...' She left the sentence unfinished.

Tony stiffened next to her. 'I see. And does the gentleman reciprocate your feelings?'

She blinked away the tears. 'I did not claim to have feelings. It would be most insensible of me, at my age, to base everything on "feelings." Instead, I had hopes.'

'Oh,' he said, clearly not understanding at all.

'He is a gentleman, his income is not as great as my late husband's nor his estates as fine, nor his title as prestigious. But, truly, I do not expect to find the equal of Robert. My first marriage was extremely fortunate in that regard. Lord Endsted was more than rich enough. And he seemed interested. Of course, they all seem interested, at first.'

'I should think that they would be. You are a charming and attractive woman, your Grace. Any man would be honoured to have your attention.' He opened his mouth, ready to say more, then stopped and looked at her. 'But I take it, the man of your choosing is not among them?'

She shook her head. 'As I said before, this is not

so much about what I choose, or what I feel. I would have been more than willing, should he have offered, or any of the others. It would have been most foolish of me to say nay if he'd have offered matrimony. But he saw me with you, and then Barton was here, when we returned. And he now thinks me inappropriate company.'

Anthony exploded with an oath. 'He does not want you because other men find you attractive? Then the man is a jealous fool. Or blind. I will find him and call him out.'

'Don't be absurd.' She laid a hand on his arm. 'He offended me, not you. And if you wish to call out every gentleman who has disappointed me, then I would have to make you a rather long list. I expect it to grow even longer, ere I find a man who will do otherwise. You came upon me in a low mood, that is all. I had not expected, at thirty, to be so thoroughly on the shelf with regard to matrimony. And I am not yet to the point where I find the other suggestions to be flattering.'

'I should think not,' he responded indignantly. 'The cheek of these men. I had thought that one such as yourself, fair as any of the young ladies of the *ton*, but with grace and poise, with wit as well as intelligence…' He showed signs of continuing, and then looked down. 'I would have thought that one such as you would have no end of suitors.'

'I have had suitors enough.' She smiled sadly. 'But

they are rarely seeking a wife. I suppose it is a comfort to know that men still find me desirable.'

'Oh, I must say yes, you are very much that. But that they would be so coarse as to suggest…'

She stared at him. 'You yourself had admitted that you would have me, should I be so inclined. I fail to see the source of your indignation on my behalf.'

'But that is before I realised that you would settle for nothing less than marriage.' He dropped to his knees before her. 'I am ever your servant, your Grace. You would do me a great honour, should you give me your hand, and I would endeavour to keep you in comfort and safety for the rest of your days.'

She pulled her hand from his grasp. 'And now you are taunting me with my foolishness.'

'I assure you, I am not. If you cannot find another who suits you, and do not wish to accept any of the other base offers made to you, then have me.'

'Most certainly not.' She had blurted out the words before she could stop to think how they might sound.

He looked up at her, eyes glazed with shock, and skin white, but with a streak of colour on each cheek as though she had slapped him hard. 'May I ask why?'

'I should think that would be obvious.'

His voice was steady, but strangely distant. 'Not to me.'

She ducked her head so that he might not see the fear in her eyes. 'We hardly know each other.'

'I doubt you knew the other gentlemen so well as you thought, if you were surprised when none of them offered. So that is not the real reason, is it?'

'All right. If you insist.' She steeled herself and said the words, 'You are a criminal. How could you expect me to accept that fact, and bind myself to you? You would ask me to live in comfort off ill-gotten gains and feel no guilt about it?'

He rose from his knees and dropped back into the seat beside her. There was a flash of pain in his eyes, but when he spoke, his colour was returning to normal and his voice was light, albeit with a slight edge of sarcasm. 'Women I have supported in the past took care not to know where the money came from. They assumed, correctly, that someone would take care of them, and shield them from the unpleasantness of finances.' He looked at her. 'Just as I assumed that, since you took the first money, and had no problem with the theft of the deed, you would not be bothered with the rest.'

'You assumed incorrectly. I take pride in knowing the details of my finances, although I cannot say I've done a very good job with them. And I am tired of men who promise to be a shield against unpleasantness, since unpleasantness has managed to find me in any case.'

'You would not have the details of it rubbed under your nose. I do not entertain my fence at my rooms. I keep my private life very much removed from my professional one.'

'Or you will until such time as you are caught and hanged. Then you will drag those around you to disgrace as well.'

The words pained him, and his voice was quiet when he responded. 'It is not as if I have never considered the fact. And I have taken great care not to be caught. Another reason I never married, I think.'

'It was probably wise of you. I cannot imagine a crueller fate for a woman than to know such a thing about her husband and to live in fear of his discovery. I could not bear it.'

A shadow passed over his face again. 'Thank you for making your opinions clear on the matter. I intended no disrespect. I only wished to offer you a solution to a problem that seems to weigh most heavily upon you. The offer stands, of course, for I doubt that my attraction for you will wane. But I will not break my heart over your refusal, since I suspect there is nothing to be done to change your low opinion of me.' His tone was light, and he seemed to have returned to normal, but she could tell he did not speak the whole truth.

'Thank you for your understanding.'

'And thank you for your honesty.' There was more than a touch of bitterness in the word. 'And tell me, does your refusal of my more noble offer extend to my friendship as well?'

'No.' Her voice was small and unsteady.

'Because I will not trouble you with my presence

again, if you find my criminality so offensive.' She had hurt him again, and she felt her resolve wavering. But she could not very well marry him, just to spare his feelings. Why could he not understand that one of them must hurt, no matter what path she chose?

She reached out to take his hand again. 'No. Please, do not forsake me. I cannot help the way I feel. I wish I could, in so many ways, and yet, I cannot. I know I cannot marry you. But neither am I able to let you go. And I do not know what I am to do, in either case. It hurts me to think of it, just as it hurt to say it aloud. And that is why I was crying.'

He laid his other hand over hers and squeezed it tightly. And his smile was sad, but it was a real smile. 'That is all right. I did not think you would say yes, and yet I felt moved to ask. I do not wish to make you cry, and am sorry to have done so. And truly, I have no desire to leave you and will not unless you send me away.'

He sighed. 'So let us not think overlong on the details of this, since they pain us both. Until such time as you say otherwise, I am yours to command, your Grace, and that should be more than enough to be happy on, I think.' And he pulled her close to him, so that she could lay her head on his shoulder, and rocked her in his arms until she dozed.

When she awoke, he was gone.

Chapter Eleven

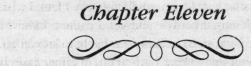

She returned to the house, lightheaded from her nap in the sunlight and unsure of her emotions. The crying had left her with a megrim that the nap had only partly soothed.

But it had been so restful, leaning against Tony, that she had quite forgotten what a bad idea it was to do so. And strange that he'd even allowed it. He had offered. She had refused. Afterwards, one of them should have slunk away in embarrassment, to nurse their wounds in private.

But he had been very accepting of her refusal, even though she could tell he was hurt. It would have been much easier if he had raged and stormed and then left her in peace. If he had abandoned her, she might have begun the difficult process of forgetting him, rather than closing her eyes and leaning into his shoulder, losing herself in a dream of what it might be like if they were two different people and she could say yes to him.

It could not have hurt him too deeply, then. It was a blow to the ego, of course. No man wanted to be told that he was not good enough to be marriage material. But it must not have been a blow to the heart. If it had been a mortal wound, he would not have recovered so quickly. It might actually have been the answer he wanted to hear, since he had done his best to help her, but had been able to keep his heart free, in case he ever managed to succeed with his dream woman.

All the more reason not to marry him. Although he might want her, he did not truly love her. Their marriage might have been a very workable relationship, if she had had the sense not to fall in love with him before he had asked. But if she had agreed to marry him because she loved him, she could see a grim future ahead. Once he had her, his ardour would cool and he would lose interest. And she would sit like the fool she was, suffering with every small indifference and worrying the night away that he would be captured and killed, or, worse yet, unfaithful.

He would be baffled by her behaviour, since he had given her no reason for it. He had made no grand promises of undying faithfulness before the marriage. Why should she expect them after?

So, it was all for the best. As long as she ignored the emptiness she felt, after denying him.

'Your Grace.' Susan rushed to her side, as she entered the house, trying to stop her as she walked down the corridor. 'I am sorry. I tried. But his foot was in the door. And when I tried to close it, he pushed me and I fell. And I told him you were not at home, but he would not go away.'

The words were overwhelming, and made no sense, but Constance knew, before she opened the door to her sitting room, who she would find there.

Barton was smiling the same placid smile he always did when dealing with her, as though common sense and reason would eventually lead her to do the unspeakable. He did not rise as she entered, remaining relaxed and in control. 'You ignored my note to you.'

'Yes, I did,' she responded. 'And my servants were instructed not to open the door for you. You cannot continue to force your way into my home, Lord Barton.'

'Your home.' When he said it, it was no longer a question. He must know that she'd got the deed.

She pretended to ignore the fact. 'I will have no more of these nonsensical threats of yours. I have no intention of becoming your mistress. And I do not acknowledge your ownership of my home. If you think you have a case, then take me to court, and prove that you own this house.'

He laughed. 'You are beautiful, Constance, and more clever than I gave you credit for. I know you have taken the deed. I don't suppose you would care to en-lighten me on how that might have happened. I suspect that the one who helped you might have another mo-tive to gain entry to my house. And I would like a word with him.'

'I do not know what you are talking about.'

'Of course you don't, darling. To hear you, I am al-most convinced. I doubt that you have the necessary skills to achieve this yourself. I know you had help. So I will watch you closely, and watch the men who watch you, until I see who your favourite shall be. And when I have discovered him, I will deal with him as he deserves.'

'My favourite? I have no favourite.'

'Not that I have noticed. But if you do not, you soon shall. The man that got the deed to your house made you work for it, I'll wager, just as I intend to.'

She almost responded that Tony had been different, before she could help herself.

He smiled as he saw the look in her eyes. 'You al-most told me. But no matter. You will slip eventually. With a word. A glance. A chance meeting that is no chance. I will find him, and punish him. If it matters to you, you might warn him that I wish him to stay out of my business and that if he thinks he can take you from me, he is sadly mistaken.' He looked up at her and reached into his pocket, producing a packet of papers. 'I took the liberty of going up to your room as you slept in the garden, and retrieving what he took from me. And thus, we are back to where we started. You owed me then, and you owe me now.'

'You lie.' She reached to snatch it from his hand, and it disappeared again, inside his coat.

'It was in the drawer of the night table, in your room. It is no trouble, getting by your servants, Constance. Freddy has kept anyone of value in his service. And you, with your soft heart, have employed his cast-offs. You are left with foolish girls and old men. It did not take more than a single blow to dispense with the few that stood in my way.'

'You struck my servants?' she said, with horror.

'I taught them who the master of this house is to be. I doubt I will have to teach them twice.'

'You had no right. They were doing their duty to me. You were trying to enter my room without permission.'

'Then you had best give them permission to obey me, or next time I will strike them harder.'

'If you must hit anyone, then hit the person who gave them the command.' She stood in front of him, daring him to raise his hand to her.

'And what good would that do, other than to mark that which I wish to remain unblemished? You are much more likely to obey me to save others, than you would to save yourself. Allow me to demonstrate. Call your maid into the room.'

'I most certainly will not.'

He got up, stepped out into the hall and said, 'Susan, come here, please. Your mistress needs you.'

'I do not!' But even as she said it, the girl had obeyed the first command, and come to the door of the sitting room. Barton seized her by the wrist and hauled her into the room, closing the door behind her.

Susan struggled, but was no match for him and he pulled her arm until her hand was held high above the flame of a candle. 'At this height, she barely feels the heat.' He pulled her arm lower, and the maid closed her eyes. 'At this height, she is beginning to feel some discomfort. It is very warm on the skin, is it not? Answer me, Susan.'

The girl nodded.

He looked again at Constance. 'Any lower, and the flesh will burn. Would you like me to demonstrate, or are you willing to see the value of co-operation?'

'You cannot do this. I will call the Runners.'

'Afterwards, perhaps. And what good will it do poor Susan then? If you try to leave the room, I will have cooked the flesh of her hand before you can return with help.'

'Let her go.'

'Give me the key to this house.'

Constance saw the resolve in his eyes and hurried to her desk, fumbling in the drawer for a spare key. Her hand trembled as she handed it to him.

He released the maid. 'Very good. We have an

understanding. And if you have a notion to bar the door against me or change the locks, know that the next time I come, I shall bring servants of my own, and it will go worse for all inside.'

He smiled thoughtfully. 'And now, let us return to the matter of your lover, the thief. He is your lover, is he not? I suspect you traded that lovely body of yours for his assistance. You should not have done that, for you knew to whom you belonged when you went to him.'

He sighed. 'And so, I will find him. And I will punish him for taking something that belongs to me. But how I punish him might well depend on how co-operative you are. I could be moved to leniency, if you treat me well and give me no more trouble. A light beating, perhaps, just as a warning. Or would you like to refuse me again, and see the consequences of your actions?' He leaned close and whispered, 'I will make him suffer. He will die screaming, and I will make sure that you hear it. Does that move you?'

'You would not dare.'

'Oh, I think so. The man is meddling in things far more important than the fate of your honour. I do not like my privacy invaded. And I do not like one to stand between me and that which I most desire. If you have any feeling at all for the man, you will warn him off, and submit to me. Or do as you please and let him feel the consequence of it. What is your decision?'

She felt her stomach drop, and she trembled. She

looked at Barton's eyes, willing them to be less heartless than they were, to give her any indication that he was not as dangerous as he appeared.

He was still smiling. 'I'm waiting. Is your continued freedom worth the cost?'

By denying Barton, she had stumbled into a situation that was well over her head and now she was dragging others down with her. 'If I agree to what you want, you will not harm him?'

'When next you see him, tell him that you are finished with him, that you belong to me, now. And that he must cease meddling in my affairs. If he leaves me alone, he will escape unharmed. If he continues to interfere, I offer no guarantees. I suggest you be very persuasive, if you have the opportunity.'

She swallowed. 'All right.'

He smiled again. 'You will find you have made a wise decision. We will dine out this evening. Vauxhall Gardens. Wear something festive. I do not wish to see you in mourning. Red, I think. And the rubies.'

A scarlet woman, she thought.

'When we have had supper, I will return here, to spend the rest of the night. Tell your maid that we are not to be disturbed.'

He rose, reaching for his hat. 'And, Constance…?'

'Yes, Lord Barton?'

'From now on, you will call me Jack. And when I take my leave, you will kiss me as if you mean it.'

He stood in the doorway, waiting.

And she stepped close to him, put her arms around his neck, and kissed him as if a life depended on it.

Chapter Twelve

Tony dropped into the wing chair in his study, staring pensively into the fire before him. He was not moved to work on the lock, though he knew he must. He wanted nothing more than to sit in the gathering darkness, alone, for the rest of his life, if need be. Would that the end were not too distant.

Patrick, sensing his mood, brought the tray with the brandy.

Tony poured a snifter for himself and waved the rest away. 'It is over,' he said.

'How so?'

'I have proposed to her, and she has refused.'

'This is most sudden.'

'It seemed like the right thing to do at the time. She hid from me, when I tried to visit her. And when I found her in the garden, she was crying. Patrick, I was defenceless. It seems that other men are offering for her in ways that are less than honourable, and she longs for matrimony. I offered my services in that department, and they were firmly declined.'

'Even after she knew who you were?'

'The matter of my identity did not come up,' Tony muttered.

'Did not…' Patrick sank into the wing chair on the opposite side of the fire, and poured himself a glass of his master's brandy. 'You expected her to take you, sight unseen, on a very limited acquaintance, and are surprised that she turned you down.'

'She seemed willing to accept many other gentlemen, with little previous acquaintance, as long as they had money or position. And before I offered, I gave her a fair description of our childhood together. There were enough clues that, had she cared to, she could have seen the truth.

'But it does not matter, whether she knows me or not. It is the reason she gave, not the denial itself that creates the problem. She said she could not marry a thief.'

Patrick shrugged and sipped his brandy. 'Then the answer is simple. If you want the girl, stop stealing.'

'There is the little detail of ten years of crime.'

Patrick waved his hand. 'Immaterial to the discussion. How much have you personally profited from it?'

Tony considered. 'Very little. When I began I had a

small inheritance, and I invested it well. But it was in no way enough to support the family. So I stole. And since I enjoyed stealing, I continued. But my own money is still there, should I choose to retire.'

'So you did not steal for yourself. You stole for others. And when you steal now?'

'There is really no cause for it, other than to cover the activities I perform for Stanton.'

'So you are, in effect, stealing for the Crown,' Patrick reasoned.

'I cannot very well tell her that, though, can I? It defeats the purpose of covert activities, if one goes trumpeting them about the neighbourhood.'

'But you are not exactly trumpeting about the neighbourhood, if you reveal the truth to one person. Or do you not trust her to keep a confidence?'

He glared at Patrick. 'I would trust her with my life. I already have. For she knows the truth about me, and has had the power to ruin me for several weeks. If she wished me ill, she had but to say something before now, to see me carted off to Newgate.'

'Then reveal the better part of your occupation, since you have revealed the worst and not come to ill. Along with your true name and history, of course,' Patrick added.

There was an annoying emphasis on the last bit of advice, and Tony chose to ignore it. 'Perhaps when I have run Barton to ground... There are risks involved. He is a dangerous man, if Stanton is to be believed.'

'All the more reason to tell her the whole truth, since she was involved with him before you entered the picture. It is the curate in you speaking again, sir. Humility does you no credit when you are using it to mask cowardice. And that is what it is. While you think nothing of staring death in the face while attempting a burglary, you stick at speaking the truth to Constance Townley since you are convinced that, once she knows who you are, she will reject you. But since she has already done that, sir, the worst is over.'

Tony readied a response, and then checked himself. What did he have to lose, after all, in telling her everything? 'Much as it pains me to have a valet who continually points out my stupidity, you are right again, Patrick. It can be no more dangerous to her than it was at the beginning, when Stanton believed her an accomplice in treason. And whatever she thinks of me, I cannot let her go blundering about, where she might thwart my schemes, or put her own freedom at risk by inadvertently aiding Barton in his plans.'

And if revealing his reason for robbing Barton raised her estimation of him? He could not help smiling at the thought.

Tony knocked firmly on the front door of Constance's house, hoping for better results in the evening than he had achieved in the afternoon. He had spent an embarrassingly long time on his toilet. His boots were polished to mirror brightness, his coat was fresh from Weston. His cravat was sublime. He had forced Patrick to shave him so close that he suspected he was missing a layer of skin, but his cheek was soft.

He hoped to be able to demonstrate the fact to Constance later in the evening.

She would be home, of course. He knew for a fact that there were no balls, soirées, or *musicales* of any value that evening—if there had been, he'd have been invited to them. His original plan had been for a quiet evening at home with a glass of port and his new safe, until he realised that Constance would be having a quiet evening at home as well. He had rehearsed his speech in his head, willing himself to stick to the plan and not be dazzled by the fineness of her eyes or the nearness of her lips. He would find her, and beg an audience. She would entertain him in the sitting room and they would chat casually of things that had nothing to do with Barton or her financial state.

He would make it clear over the course of the evening that his interest had nothing to do with the business of the deed, and everything to do with the high esteem in which he held her. In which any sane and decent man could not help but hold her.

He would explain his current interest in Barton, his present occupation and the relative safety of it, compared with his life of a year ago, when he had been stealing full time. Should he ever be caught now, Stanton would manage to free his neck from the noose and explain all. While it was not without scandal, and not so honourable as a title and land, it was not such a horrible thing as she imagined and she would not be embarrassed, should the whole truth of it come to light.

And then he would explain to her that they were not the strangers she might think them, and that it would make him the happiest man on earth if only she would consent to marry him.

But he remembered the kisses and the way she'd responded to them and changed his plan.

He would tell her that it would make him the happiest man on the planet if she might consent to marry him tomorrow, and consent tonight to everything else. Because he was quite mad with desire for her, and had been so for as long as he could remember. And there was little hope of him progressing with the Barton matter or anything else until he'd had her.

He grinned at the thought. Doubts presented themselves, of course. He had lacked the nerve to strike when the iron was hottest, the woman in his arms, and the bed scant paces away.

But he remembered the previous night, the way she had clung to him, when he had turned to go, and asked if she would see him again with such sweet hope in her eyes. That must have been more than gratitude. She might deny him in daylight, but the sun was down and his luck was about to change.

The maid, Susan, opened the door, and he was surprised to see fear in her eyes before she recognised him. And then, as she always did, she told him her mistress was not at home.

'Susan, let us have no more of that tonight. Be honest with me. Is she not at home, truly, or is she not at home to me?'

Susan was looking at him as though she expected him to eat her. 'Not at home, sir.'

'Because I will hear no more nonsense on the subject, from you, or from her. If she is hiding in her bedroom, or the garden, or any other room in the house, you are to go to her immediately and tell her I wish to speak to her, just for once, in the parlour over a cup of tea, like a civilised gentleman. Tell her, if you would, that I have fallen off the ivy and twisted my ankle, and will not leave her sitting room until it is healed.'

Susan now looked both baffled and terrified.

'It is a lie, of course,' he assured her. 'My ankle is fine, as is the ivy. But say anything you need to, to get her down out of her room.'

'I cannot, sir.'

'Can you say it for a crown, then?'

'Sir!'

'A guinea?'

'I cannot...'

'A five-pound note, Susan. Name your price, and I will pay, but you will not put me off.'

She ignored the money in his hand, closed her eyes and said, 'Mr Smythe. I will not take your money, for it will mean disobeying my mistress. And she said I am, under no circumstances, to tell you that she has gone out this evening, to Vauxhall, with Lord Barton. If you arrive, I am to do whatever is necessary to get you to leave this house so that you are not here when they return for the evening.' Susan seemed no happier saying the words than he was in hearing them.

He could feel the muscles of his smile tightening to a rictus. 'Thank you, Susan. I will not seek her here, then. I feel the need of some night air. Perhaps a trip to the Gardens.'

'Thank you, sir,' Susan whispered. 'And be careful. He's a bad 'un.' And she closed the door to him.

The glitter of Vauxhall at night was lost on Tony, as he paid his admission to enter. Acres of land, much of it secluded walkways. How was he to find her in the throng of revellers present? He must trust that Barton meant to keep her where she could be seen, since there was little point in stepping out with her if he did not intend for them to be noticed.

Tony scanned the crowds in the avenues, and the people gathered around the tightrope walker, and worked his way around the dance floor near the orchestra until a flash of crimson caught his eye. She was there, on Barton's arm.

She was stunning, as only she could be. He had grown quite used to seeing her about town in mourning, or half-mourning, but even after her recent return to fashion, he had not seen her looking so splendid as this. The deep red of her gown made her skin glow luminous in the lantern light, her dark hair was dressed with tiny red roses, and her throat and ears were adorned with pigeon's-blood rubies that would have left the thief in him quivering with excitement, had the man in him not been more interested in seeing the bare skin beneath.

The image of her as she had been when she came to his rooms was still burning in his mind: the true outline of the body hidden just under the satin. There was the swell of her breast and the place where the nipple would raise the fabric of the gown, and there was the curve of her stomach, and the place where the gown would pool where her legs met. Her cruelty knew no bounds if she had revealed herself to him in that way only to give herself to another.

But now Barton was escorting her along the dim pathways, deeper and deeper into the dark walks of Vauxhall Gardens.

Tony knew the reason that a gentleman might escort a lady into the grounds, for he had done it himself. But the ladies were rarely ladies, nor did the gentlemen have any intention of keeping to manners.

Her dark eyes were unreadable and her face revealed neither joy nor sadness. She was as cool and aloof as any of the statues adorning the garden walkways. After all the fine talk of marriage and reputation earlier in the day, she showed no sign of caring how her behaviour must look to any who saw it tonight.

The couple disappeared around a bend on the darkened path, and Tony hopped the nearest hedge and cut across the grass, staying out of the glow of the lanterns to keep pace with them as they proceeded. Around him, on other paths in the darkness, he could hear the sounds of other couples: giggles, sighs and the occasional moan.

And a few yards away from him, Barton had stopped, and pulled Constance close to speak into her ear.

She was leaning into him and looking up into his face, and when he whispered to her, she did not pull away. She glanced around, to see if there was anyone following.

Tony stepped further into the darkness to be sure that he was hidden.

When she was sure they were alone, she kissed Barton quickly on the lips.

The bastard tilted his head and spoke again.

And again she kissed, more slowly this time, with her sweet mouth open to his. It was nothing like the kisses Tony had seen between them, in Barton's own garden. That night, she had been awkward and it had appeared that she could barely tolerate the man she was with.

Tonight, she was kissing him with her whole spirit, her body tight against his, her arms clutching his shoulders.

Tony's heart sank. Had anyone noticed the pair together, other than him? Most probably not. It was Vauxhall, after all, and the other couples walking these paths had secrets of their own to keep and no time to pry.

But Constance must have known what would happen if she came here. Why would she let Barton take such a liberty, after the way she had acted in her rooms, and his?

She had said that Barton had the deed to her house. And she had offered her body in trade to Tony if he could get it back.

But had she truly said that Barton's attentions were unwelcome? Tony swallowed. Perhaps he had misunderstood. It was only the theft of the deed that was unwelcome. If she owned the house, she could invite who she chose to share her bed: him, or Barton or anyone else.

So perhaps what Stanton had first claimed was the truth. She was a faithless traitor, with no more loyalty to Barton than to anyone else.

The thought made him ache.

And yet, he could not stop wanting her. He had wanted her all the time she was married, he had wanted her before that, he had wanted her when they were children, before he even knew what he wanted her for. And because he was a fool, he would continue to want her, if she belonged to Barton or married another. It was lucky that he had not told her when he'd had the chance, or she'd have known the strength of her hold over him and left him with even less dignity than he already possessed.

But if he could not have her, the least he could do was get her clear of Barton before the man's inevitable destruction.

The garden was as it ever was, gay and enchanting in the darkness. Robert had disapproved of Vauxhall, saying it attracted too common a crowd, but the few times she had gone, she had found it strangely exciting to be able to mingle with royalty and courtesans, watching the entertainments, and listening to the orchestra while eating overpriced ham sandwiches and drinking cheap wine. The pavilions glittered with gilt and mirrors. There was dancing and laughter all around her. And later, there would be fireworks.

She doubted she would be there to see them, for she would be home, in bed. With Barton. He had already led her down one of the dark walks so that they might kiss. She tried not to think of it as a preamble to what was coming. At least it had not been quite so horrible as when she had admitted defeat and kissed him in the sitting room, earlier that day.

This time, she had been able to close her mind to who she was with, imagining that she had been lured down a walk by another who wished to pull her into the darkness, a few steps away from the familiar world, and kiss her to insensibility.

And she had gone willingly, for after a few glasses of wine, the familiar world had seemed intolerably dull, and wickedness in the darkness of Vauxhall excited her.

When she was sure they were alone, she had kissed Barton once, and asked to go back to the dancing. But he had told her that she would need to try much harder. So she had closed her eyes and thought of how different it might be if she were here with Tony. And a few minutes later, Barton had pulled away and declared himself pleased with her response and led her back towards the light.

When they neared the orchestra pavilion, she requested another glass of wine, and he left her alone in the crowd to go find her refreshment. She suspected it would take many more glasses to get through the evening, but it would be worth any price to settle Barton's vicious temper until she could think of a better plan.

The music began again. It was to be a waltz. She looked around her with resignation. Barton would return and claim her for a dance. She had been lucky so far, and seen no one familiar. But if any who knew her were present, there would be talk. It could not be helped.

A hand from the crowd seized hers and pulled her

out on to the floor. And she found herself not in the arms of Barton, but staring into the face of Anthony Smythe, inches from her own.

'There, now. Did I not promise you that you would run into me at many gatherings, now that you know me? And here the truth is proved, for you are waltzing with me.'

She looked over her shoulder, in panic. 'I had promised this dance to another.'

'I suspect it is Barton, for he is coming towards us and looks most furious.'

She struggled to escape from Tony's grasp. 'He must not see us together.'

Tony's grip held tight and he pulled her closer. 'I do not see how he can help it, for we are together before his very eyes.'

She stared into the crowd, looking for Barton, sick with dread of what was to come.

'Do not search after other men, when you are in my arms. I find it most damaging to the spirit to think I cannot hold your attention for the space of a single dance.' His tone hardened. 'Particularly if you must look at Barton. I had hoped, after what I needed to do for you last week, and all the fine talk in the garden about wanting an honourable marriage, that you would have the sense to stay away from him.'

'I could not help myself,' she admitted with honesty.

'Nor could you the last time. You needed *my* help,

as I remember it. And were willing to go to surprising lengths to get it.'

She lifted her chin. 'And I do not need you any more.'

'You are done with me, then?'

'Yes,' she insisted. 'I wish you to leave me alone. And leave Barton alone, as well.'

'And what happened to all the pretty words about preferring my attentions to those of Barton's?'

'The situation has changed.'

'I see.' He could see exactly what she wanted him to see. He was angry. Angry enough to leave, she hoped, since she did not know how much longer she could stand to lie to him.

'I do not need your help or your company, and wish you to stay far from me in the future.'

Instead he pulled her even closer, so that her body brushed his coat front and his lips were near her ear. His voice was rough as he said, 'I will leave you, then. But before I go, let me help you one last time with a word of advice. Stay away from Barton. His star is no longer on the rise. When things come crashing down about him, I would hate to see you caught in the result.'

She felt sick and frightened and angry, all at the same time. She could go to Barton because he forced her to, only to have Smythe destroy her along with Barton. Or she could not go to Barton, and he would destroy Smythe and everyone else around her. Either way, she was trapped.

'And that is your idea of help, is it?' She slapped him on the shoulder hard enough to knock him out of step. 'And now, Mr Smythe, I will tell you what I think of your help. You have been breaking into Barton's home for reasons of your own, and only pretending to help me. But it does not really have much to do with me, does it? For you have been spying on Barton since that first day, when I caught you spying on me. You claim you want to help, and you pretend to be different. But you are no different than Barton is. First you flatter, then you steal, and if you are not successful, you try blackmail. And at last, you resort to threats to make me do as you wish.'

'Threats?' He pushed her away so that he could look down into her eyes, trying to read the truth in them until she was forced to look away to hide it. 'He is threatening you still?' The hand that held hers squeezed her fingers and he pulled her close again. 'Why did you not just tell me? When I saw you together, I thought... Well, never mind what I thought. I was a fool.' He glanced at the musicians. 'The dance will be ending soon. Tell Barton whatever you like: that I forced you to dance or that you went willingly to spite him. Then, the first chance you get, lose yourself in the crowd. Do not go to him tonight, no matter what he is holding over your head. And I will be sure he does not come to you. You needn't be afraid of him or do anything that you do not wish to do. I can still help you, if you will let me. Why did you not ask?'

She thought of Barton's threats, and what might happen to Tony if she involved him again. 'The last time, what I asked you to do was wrong. I can not ask it again. It is too dangerous.'

He leaned forward and laughed in her ear. 'It is in my nature to do wrong. There is very little you can do to redeem my character other than to allow me to use my more improper talents in a good cause. What you asked was no imposition, and a chance to see some much-needed justice done in the world. I do not care a fig for the dangers that concern you. I will bring down Barton in any case, but I do not want my actions to injure you, for you are innocent of his villainy. If he is doing something to thwart that, then will you do me the great honour of allowing me to help you again?'

She hesitated, and he spun her around the floor so that Barton could not see them speak.

'Say the word, your Grace. I will not impose on you further, if you truly do not wish it. But if you but nod, I will come to your rooms later, and you can tell me all. Then, if you do not wish my help, send me away.'

She was almost weak with relief at the thought of talking to him, and leaned against him and let him feel the change in her body as she gave herself up to his protection.

He squeezed her hand again. 'Very well, then. Go home and unlock your window.' He smiled at her. As the music ended, he spun her back to the place she had been, to stand by the irate Barton. 'Delightful, your Grace, and so sorry to impose, but I could not resist the temptation to steal the dance.'

She watched the light of recognition flare in Barton's eyes at his choice of words.

Barton glared at him. 'You should be careful what you steal, sir. For you know what happens to thieves.'

Tony laughed. 'I have but to read *The Times* to see that, sir. Hanging. But at least it is not so bad as the thing that happens to traitors. While the courts might show leniency to a thief, counterfeiting is high treason. To be hanged, drawn and quartered for acting against your own country?' Tony shuddered theatrically. 'A nasty end, is it not, Jack?'

Barton's normal composure broke, and he grew even angrier than he had been; his cold smile turned to a grimace of fury and his colouring was mottled red. 'Then a traitor need have no reason to fear doing murder, Smythe. The slow and painful death of another will add nothing to the severity of the punishment, should one be caught.'

She reached out and tugged Barton's sleeve to distract him, and he shook her off.

Tony tipped his head to one side, considering. 'I suppose it would not, if one could manage such a feat. But in your case, I have my doubts. Shall we see?' And he turned and started towards the dark walks.

And Barton cursed once, and made to follow. Then

he turned back to her. 'You are to return home immediately, go to your room, and wait for me there.'

She grabbed his arm. 'I will do nothing of the kind. I know what you mean to do. And you promised you would not.'

Tony turned back and looked at her curiously. 'Do as he says, Constance. Go home. Whatever occurs, I do not wish you to be a part of it. Do you understand?'

She looked between the two men, both implacable. 'Go.' Barton pointed towards the exit as though ordering a dog to its kennel.

'Please, your Grace,' Tony added.

And then he walked away, in the direction of the most secluded paths, disappearing into the nearest crowd.

Barton followed.

Chapter Thirteen

Constance sat on the end of her bed, knotting and unknotting her handkerchief in quaking hands. Why had she listened to either of them? She should have thrown herself onto Barton and held him back.

But Tony had gone so quickly and left Barton to push and shove his way through a group of people. When she had gone after him, she had been swept along with the group, and was near to the exit before she got clear, having seen no sign of Tony or Barton.

She had searched for a while, but been afraid to venture into the darkness alone, and finally had hired a hackney and hurried back to her house, shooed the maid away, locked the door and unlocked the window. Please, dear Lord, let it be Tony who arrived and not Barton. She did not think she could bear the sight of him, much less his touch, if she knew that he had come to her rooms with Tony's blood on his hands.

'By your leave, your Grace?' Tony stood framed in the open window, awaiting her permission to enter.

'Oh, do not be such a fool. Come in before someone sees you.' She rushed to the window and reached to pull him in herself, patting at his chest with her hands, searching for some sign of injury.

He stepped into her room as easily as if he'd entered it from the hall, laughing as her hands touched him, catching them and bringing them to his lips. 'You thought I would come to harm from Barton?'

She looked at him incredulously. 'I was terrified. You must have known what I would think.'

'That I would go into the darkness and let him brawl with me, in a public park? Not knowing who he might have brought with him for aid or what trap might await me? I'm sorry to disappoint you, darling, but I ran like a rabbit until I was quite sure he was lost on the paths, and then I came here. And I can assure you; I am quite unharmed.' He placed her hands against his chest again. 'But you may touch me as much as you like. I find it most pleasant.'

She snatched her hands away and turned from him. 'I was a fool to agree to this. I should never have allowed you to come. I put you at risk for helping me, and you treat it as if it were a joke. But I thought you deserved a warning. Barton knows I had help getting the deed. And yesterday he forced his way into my home and took it back. After tonight, he must know it was you who helped me. He wants revenge. He means to hurt you.'

Anthony laughed. 'I gathered that. I wish him luck in it.'

'Do not talk that way. You do not understand what he is capable of.'

He smiled. 'I am sorry, but so many men have threatened me over the years. I am still here, and quite whole.' He stood before her, hands outspread, inviting another examination. When she did not reach for him, he became serious again. 'I thank you for the warning, although I am not particularly concerned by Barton's threats. And what might all that have to do with your kissing him in a public place?'

'You saw?'

'Indeed. You were not enjoying it? Because you appeared most enthusiastic.' His smile was gone, and his tone demanded an explanation.

'What choice do I have? He gave me a demonstration yesterday of the depths he is willing to stoop to ensure my obedience. He beat my servants. He tortured my maid before my very eyes, until I gave him the key to my house. And threatened to do the same to you if I did not submit to him.

'He has everything, and yet he wants more from me. I have no money, no power in this. But I cannot allow him to hurt you. And he would, since he knows how it might hurt me.' Her hands had begun to shake and her breathing was becoming unsteady. If she did not get hold of herself, she would be gasping, and the gasps would turn to sobs. And she feared the crying would never stop.

'And why did you not come to me when I asked you to?' His voice was gentle.

'He is watching me. Every move I make. He was waiting for me to go to you, so that… He said…' She closed her eyes. 'That he would know who helped me, because I would go to him, or he would come to me, just as you did tonight. And when he found you out, he would get back at you. It would go hard for you, but it would go harder still if I did not co-operate. He said that I must tell you he knows what you are seeking more than the deed. He will kill you, if you try again. There might be clemency, if I do as he says. But if I resist, he will take pleasure in hurting you, and that I should know that it would be all my fault.' She stared at him, willing him to understand enough to be worried.

But he laughed. 'That is all, then?'

'Tonight, when we danced, he suspected. And then you taunted him and removed all doubt. How could you be so foolish?'

'I could not help it. He stood there, all puffed up like an angry red balloon. It was too tempting to deflate him.'

'You called him traitor.'

'Because he is one,' Tony replied simply.

'And so you know he has nothing to lose. He is angrier still and will be watching us both. For all I know he has followed you here tonight.'

'He did not follow me,' he reassured her. 'No one knows I am here. You need have no fear of it.'

She smiled in relief. 'If he does not know where to find you, then you are safe for now. But he must know your direction. He will try to find you there. He may be waiting for you at your home, even now.'

'Very astute of you. That is exactly where he is. I followed him to my home and have seen him, watching my house. I left him catching a chill on the street corner, waiting for me to return, so that he could do me mischief. And I have set a man of my own to watch the watcher. If Barton moves from the spot, he will not get far.'

She reached out to clasp his hand. 'Then you can get away. Leave from here. Leave tonight. Get out of the country. Go to the Continent, or perhaps the Americas. I do not care. But swear to me that you will be far away from here by morning, so that I need have no fear for you.'

He smiled and shook his head. 'And what will become of you, if I leave?'

'He does not mean to hurt me. He has assured me of that.'

'He will be quite public about keeping you, and everyone will know it. Think of what you will lose, Constance. Your friends. The prospects you held so dear, even this morning. All of it will be gone.'

'Honour is only an idea. It will not hurt to lose it. I am no innocent, Tony. I know what must be done, and it means nothing, compared to your life. It does not matter to me, as long as I know you are safe.'

'You would be willing to ruin yourself, to preserve my miserable hide?' His eyes were serious. Then his face spread in a lazy grin, but he showed no sign of taking his leave. 'On the contrary, I think it matters a great deal.'

'Not to me. Not any more. I will go to him if I must. If that is what it takes to keep you safe. But you must leave him alone. Whatever you are after, do not seek it in his house. Has no one told you that it is wrong to steal? It was only a matter of time before you met someone like Barton, who was worse than you and could punish you for your crimes.'

He waved the argument aside, his grin wide and without care. 'Leave off with your begging, for I am not moving from this spot until I am good and ready. But tell me again, because I love to hear you say it— you do not go to him by choice?'

'Of course not. The man is horrid.'

'And you are only tolerating his attentions to protect me?' he prompted.

'I cannot let this go any further. He will not have you, if there is anything I can do to prevent it.'

Anthony sighed and fixed her with his smile. 'I cannot tell you how relieved I am to hear that. I thought your problem was something serious, or difficult. Or that you secretly fancied Barton and were using me to control him. But you are trying to save me?' He laughed. 'And that is all? Do not worry. You need do nothing. I will take care of everything.'

She paced the room, wringing her handkerchief in her hands. 'You will go back out the window to search his rooms, and I am to stay here and wait for a report of your death? I vow, your offer of assistance is most welcome, but there is nothing you can do that will not put you in greater jeopardy.'

Tony replied, with gentle insistence. 'You need have no fear. Relax. Let everything to me.'

'That is what my late husband said. Do not worry, Constance. Do not be such a goose. Everything will be fine. I trusted him in all things, and look what I have come to. Barton means to have me and kill you. It is too late for me. But you can still escape him. Run, Tony. Run far away. If you come to harm because of me, I swear I shall go mad.'

He moved as silently as a cat and was upon her before she realised, taking her by the shoulders and pinning her to the wall to stop her pacing. He looked down into her face with his wild smile and dream-filled eyes, and said, 'I shall go mad, if I must watch you make another circuit of the room.' He reached behind her and caught the tie of her bodice, tugging to undo the bow. 'Although it is rather pleasant to see you so overwrought for my sake.'

'But he is a villain, Tony, and he knows about you. What are we to do? I—'

His lips came down on hers, stopping her words. The kiss was forceful, almost brutal in its intensity, and he held her tight against him, so that she could feel his body responding to her. She could feel his hands on her back, dealing, one by one, with the hooks of her dress. Then he pushed away from her, placing his hands on her shoulders, holding her tight in place. 'You shall do nothing tonight. Not with Barton, at any rate.' He trailed his fingers forward, along the gaping neckline of her dress.

'Stop it,' she muttered. 'We mustn't. There isn't time. He will come for me tonight. And if he finds you here…'

'I said—' he pushed at the fabric, and the dress slipped off her shoulders '—I would take care—' he reached behind her to undo her stays '—of everything. But if you are sure you want me to run away, then you need merely say the word, and I shall go.'

'He said—'

'Never mind Barton, for a moment. What is it that you want, your Grace?' He was trailing his fingers over the bare skin of her back and she shuddered with the shock of it.

And then his hands slipped beneath her chemise, stroking her sides, grazing her breasts. 'All things being equal, do you wish me to stay?'

She closed her eyes and tried not to think of what his touch was doing to her, and spoke. 'Of course I do not want you to go. But—'

'Stop right there.' He laid a finger on her lips. 'Do not spoil it with more talking. You have said enough. Now let me help.'

Oh, dear. She stayed very still as he worked the rest of the laces free.

It was not as if she objected. But it all would have been easier a night ago, when she was not so frightened. Tonight, passion was the last thing on her mind. But if she could be still and give herself up to Tony, she could keep him away from Barton for the rest of the night. He had been working on her behalf for quite some time and she had done nothing for him but cause him trouble. And if this was to be goodbye, she could not send him away without something.

It would be better for him if he ran, as she had told him to. She would be alone again, but he would be safe.

But she did quite miss the comfort of a man's arms around her, the soft words and gentle kisses.

He freed the corset and in one smooth move pulled it forward and away from her body and pushed her bodice and chemise to her waist. She was bare before him.

She closed her eyes, afraid of what she might see

in his eyes. She was not old, certainly, but well past her prime. Suppose it was not what he had expected? She opened her eyes to look at him.

And he did not notice, for he was gazing at her breasts in hungry fascination. He reached up to cup them in his hands, closed his eyes and sighed, and when he looked at her again his smile widened.

All right. He seemed satisfied in that. And she had to admit that even though her nerves were jangling with dread, the feel of his hands as they caressed her was more than pleasant. There was a low humming in her blood as he looked at her. She was lying to herself to pretend that it would be a hardship to submit to him. And if they did it quickly, he would still be away before Barton tumbled to his whereabouts.

She reached up and pulled his hand away, ready to lead him to her bed.

And he shook off her touch and pushed her firmly back against the wall.

Dear Lord. Did he mean to take her standing up? The humming was a singing in her at the thought. It would not take very long at all, then. Or so she thought. She had never tried it. It would be something that required more co-ordination, more balance, more stamina than she was used to in a partner. It was not something she had experience in. And was unlikely to be gen—

His lips came down on hers, stopping thought as he

took her tongue. His hands grasped her waist and found the strings of her petticoat, undid them and pushed the fabric to the floor, leaving her naked before him.

He stepped away to admire her.

She regained her thought. Gentle. He was not likely to be gentle, but she doubted that he would be so rough as to hurt her. She must need remember to relax, when the moment came, to make it easy for him to enter, and perhaps afterwards she could ask him to lie in her bed and hold her for a few minutes, before he had to go.

Did one ask for such things? She was not sure.

He was staring at her naked body, and she remembered too late that she should be embarrassed. At the very least, she should do something to help him out of his clothing, since the situation was highly unequal. She reached for the buttons of his waistcoat.

He seized her by the wrists and pinned them against the wall, and said, his face close to hers, 'I said I would take care of everything, your Grace.'

And before she could suggest that under the circumstances he might call her Constance, his mouth was on hers again. She tried to pull her hands free, but he was too strong for her and held her pinned as he took her mouth. His grip on her hands was relaxed but unmovable, and she found she quite liked the feeling of struggling against his hold, the wool of his coat rubbing against her nakedness. And the way her movements seemed to inflame his ki—

He was kissing her mouth with savage ferocity, and she writhed in his grasp, and with a shudder, she gave herself up to him, going weak and pliant in his arms. Only then did his lips move to her throat, and she could feel his tongue licking and his teeth biting at her pulse and making it jump in response. He released her hands and imprisoned her body between his and the wall, stroking down her back to cup her bottom before taking her by the shoulders and steadying himself as he lowered his mouth to her breasts.

She tried to catch her breath, now that her mouth was free, but found it impossible. His mouth was greedy and hard against her and his hands slipped to her waist and squeezed, holding her steady as he su—

Oh, dear Lord. His mouth was on her nipple, pulling hard and his hand slipped between her legs and…

She pressed her back into the wall to keep from collapsing with the shock of it. He was making love to her with his hands, caressing her legs, spreading her sex and slipping those agile fingers in and out of her. She grabbed at her own hair, and it fell in a shower of pins and rose petals, the curls forming a curtain around him as he kissed her breasts. Then she ran her fingers through the waves in his hair, clutching at the back of his neck to hold his mouth to her and urge him on. Her breath was coming faster, sensations piling on top of sensation. And then subsiding as he pulled his mouth away to…

He cupped his hand over her sex and slid to his knees before her, trailing kisses down her belly until he came to her navel, setting up a rhythm with his tongue and his hand, until she was rocking against him and pressing herself down on his hand to push his fingers more deeply into her, clutching his shoulders as though he were the only solid thing in the world.

And he stopped. He lifted his head to look up into her face, dominating her even as he knelt at her feet. And again he smiled, and this time it was in triumph as he thrust into her with one hand, grabbed her hip with the other, and pulled her to his mou…

And she lost herself, her cares, her body, and her mind, and yet the kiss did not end. She begged him to stop and in the same breath begged him for more, and he laughed against her and began it all again until her legs shook under her and she writhed against him as the feelings rolled through her again and again.

'Your Grace?'

He pulled away from her at last and laid his head against her thigh, idly kissing the soft flesh.

'Your Grace, is anything the matter?'

She shook her head, trying to understand what she was hearing.

'Because I heard you cry out.' Oh, dear, she had forgotten the maid. 'Your Grace? The door is locked. Do you need assistance?'

She leaned her head back against the wall, wondering if she could stand any more help for the evening without dying of happiness.

When Tony smiled up at her, the lazy, carefree grin was back. He bit her hip, and let his fingertips play over the back of her knees.

'Your Grace?' There was a trace of laughter in her maid's voice. It had been obvious to Susan what she had been doing. And, Constance suspected, quite loud.

'No, Susan. Do not trouble yourself. I am fine.' The maid retreated.

'You are fine. Very fine indeed,' Tony whispered against her belly. 'And I must go.'

'But you haven't—'

'But you have. Twice, at least.' He smiled with pride and rose to take her hands. 'I told you I would make it all better. I must go and take care of Barton and retrieve your deed and your keys. I suspect he is quite cold and stiff after all this time standing in the street. Whereas I feel most refreshed.' He let go of her hands and scooped her up in his arms, and she squealed in delight as he carried her to her bed and tossed her under the covers, pulling them over her naked body. 'You need not fear a visit from him tonight. Now, go to sleep, and if you would…' he kissed her '…dream of me.'

'Sleep?' How could he even suggest it?

'I have work yet to do. It is a shame, isn't it, that in my chosen profession the work begins when the sun goes down, for it leaves me less time to spend with you.'

'But you will come again,' she whispered. 'Soon. When you can stay with me.'

And he grinned. 'As your Grace pleases.'

There, he thought with some satisfaction as he climbed out of the window and gained the street. She had left off the notion that he need run for his life. In fact, he was quite sure that she would be most vehemently opposed to his going anywhere without her. And she had forgotten all about sleeping with Barton as well. Although the notion that she would make the ultimate sacrifice for him was flattering, under no circumstances would he allow her to do so.

But it gave him proof enough that he need no longer worry about Constance's feelings towards him. She might think that marriage was an impossibility. But there were many other things she seemed ready to agree to, and he would soon teach her that the advantages of becoming his wife might outweigh the negatives of birth and career.

As he approached his rooms, he saw the shadowy figure concealed in the bushes long before it saw him, which was highly amusing.

'Barton.' He smiled his most unctuous smile, and strode up to the man, clapping him on the back.

Barton started at the unexpected contact, and then straightened and failed miserably at hiding his confusion.

'Forgotten me so soon? My name is de Portnay

Smythe. I believe we spoke this evening, when I was rescuing Constance Townley from the tedium of having to waltz with you.' Tony smiled. 'I was most disappointed to lose you in the crowd at the Gardens, for I rather thought that you meant to teach me a lesson.'

Barton's eyes narrowed. 'Someone must, Smythe. It is well past time you learned that sticking your nose where it doesn't belong can be very bad for your health.'

Tony shrugged. 'Perhaps. But I doubt you will be the one to teach me, for you have not learned that lesson yourself. Your continued harassment of the Dowager Duchess of Wellford, for example, is about to prove extremely unhealthy.'

Barton smiled. 'I beg to differ. I was there first, Smythe. She did not seem the least bit harassed, when last we were alone, and I have no desire to part with her. I assure you, the lady's services are already engaged.'

Tony ignored the red haze of rage that formed at the idea of Barton alone with Constance, and sneered. 'Her services are engaged? You talk of her as though you are hiring a coach. If she were in agreement on that point, then we would have nothing to speak of here. But in talking to her, I gather she is somewhat distressed by your attentions. And so, you will cease them, immediately.'

It was Barton's turn to sneer. 'You believe that she prefers you, a low-born thief?'

Tony ignored the insult. 'Whether she might prefer me is immaterial to this discussion. We are talking of that which she does not prefer. And that would be you. Noble birth does not erase the fact that you are a criminal as well, *Lord* Barton. Perhaps, in respect to your fine blood, I should offer you the chance to settle our differences on the field of honour.' Tony laughed to himself at the idea. 'But I am just a common man. I am no fencer, sir, and not much of a shot. I will not give you a chance to stick me when the sun rises, any more than I will allow you to knife me in the back on a street corner this evening. If you think you deserve Constance Townley's affections, then prove to me that you are the better man. Try and take them from me.' He raised his hands, prepared to fight.

Barton took the stance of so many fine gentlemen, fists up to protect his noble profile.

Tony ignored it and punched him once in the stomach, watching him fold and drop to the ground. He looked down at the man who lay gasping at his feet. 'And this is why, if you wish to fight, it is better to learn it in the street, than from Gentleman Jim. You may find, Barton, that much of the prancing and preening you've been taught is quite useless against a rogue such as myself. And while you are quite terrifying to old men and ladies' maids, I find you to be a bit of a joke.'

Tony reached down, grabbed Barton by a lapel and ran a hand efficiently through the pockets of the coat, until he came upon the deed. 'Carrying it with you to prevent me from stealing it? I thought as much. And you see how well that succeeded.' He continued his search, removing more papers and a key ring. He flipped through the papers. 'Let us see what else we have. IOUs. And here is one from Constance's idiot nephew.' He stared down in disgust at Barton. 'No one is this lucky at cards, Jack. Therefore, I will surmise you cheated and will take the lot. I suspect it will be like early Christmas for the owners to get them back.'

He examined the ring of keys, removing one that fit the lock he had noticed on Constance's front door. 'You will not be needing this, and so I will return it to its owner as well.' He glared at Barton. 'A true gentleman would never accept something that was not freely given.'

He made to return the keys, and then hesitated. 'I don't suppose, while we are here together, that you would like to tell me the location of the key to your safe. I do not see it, on the ring here. It would be round, with a notched end. With a little cap to keep the dust out of the grooves.'

Barton glared up at him with murder in his eyes.

'Didn't think so.' Tony smiled. 'Never mind. I didn't really want it. I will open the lock on my own, soon enough. I enjoy the challenge, and having the key would spoil my fun. But do not think for a moment that you can succeed in your plans to mint your own money. The government is on to you, and has set me to stop you to prevent scandal. But they will have you, no matter what you do. My advice to you, as a fellow criminal, is to admit defeat, turn over the plates and run while they will still allow it.'

He tossed the other keys back into the muck of the street.

'Do you understand?'

Barton had left off gasping, and he struggled up on one hand and spat on the ground at Tony's feet.

Tony kicked the hand out from under him, rolled Barton over with the toe of his boot and planted his foot across the man's throat. 'I said, do you understand? I am concerned, predominantly, about the Duchess of Wellford. It stops here, Barton. You will leave her alone. Are we clear on that?' He increased his pressure on the man's throat.

Barton nodded with difficulty.

He removed his foot from Barton's neck, allowing the man to sit up. 'You are no doubt having thoughts right now about what you will do to me, once you get your wind back. If you mean to call me out, you will be unsuccessful, for I will laugh in your face. I am proud to be a live coward in a family of dead heroes and I do not need to duel to prove my worth. If you accost me in public, I will make it clear to all within earshot what I think of the sort of man who needs to use blackmail to gain the affections of a lady.

'And if you think, as you did tonight, that it will be possible to waylay me, alone or with the help of friends, or that it will be possible to send servants or lackeys to give me a taste of what's coming to me, then I suggest you think again. Better men than you have tried it, but none has been successful. Should you manage it, know that when I am not dealing with the likes of you, I am a likeable fellow with many friends in high places and in low. They should be unhappy, should anything happen to me, and have been warned from whom the attack is most likely to come. They will take action on my behalf should I be unable to do so.'

He smiled down at the prone man. 'Likewise, do not attempt to harass the duchess further, or seek retribution for my actions. I will take a wrong against her as a wrong committed against my own person. I believe the Italians have a word for what I intend. Vendetta. It is much what you intended for me.'

He looked down at the beaten man. 'You may consider this your last warning on the matter. I mean to finish you in any case, and will have those plates. I suggest you drop what you are planning and run, as far and as fast as you can. I will not follow, and the state is willing to let you go. But if I ever hear that you have interfered with the duchess or her household, justice will be swift and no distance great enough to protect you. Do you understand?'

Barton glared.

Anthony dug a toe into his ribs. 'Yes or no, Barton. Do you understand?'

'Yes.'

Tony smiled down at him. 'Very good. We have an understanding. Good night to you, sir. And don't make me have to do this again.'

Chapter Fourteen

Constance stretched under the sheet and enjoyed the feel of the linen on her bare body. She felt a *frisson* of desire and the memories came flooding back. In spite of herself, she smiled.

He had told her not to worry, and then he'd taken off her clothes, and pleasured her until she could bear it no more.

And then he'd put her to bed and taken his leave. She'd dreamed all night of him, lying next to her on the pillow, and it was sweet disappointment to wake and find that he wasn't there.

There was a quiet knock on the door.

It was still locked, and her maid could not get in. She wrapped the sheet around herself, then hurried to the door in bare feet and turned the key in the lock, grabbed the clothing from off the floor and tossed it over the nearest chair, trying to give the illusion that she had found her own way to bed.

Susan came in smiling, and doing her best to pretend that there was nothing unusual about her mistress's behaviour. There was an envelope, set beside the morning's hot chocolate.

Constance looked to her enquiringly.

'It was delivered this morning, your Grace, with the first post.'

She glanced down at the seal. An S, unfamiliar in its design. She slit the wax and unfolded the note. Her deed and inventory slid on to the tray.

So soon?

Obviously. She felt the last of the tension leaving her body. A short note slid from the envelope as well, and she laid it against her heart before reading.

I am safe as houses, as are you. If you would welcome a visit from one who will always be your humble servant, so that you might have return of your house key, send your maid to bed early and leave your window unlocked.

There was no signature.

She sank back into the pillows, and closed her eyes, holding the note to her lips. He had the key to her front door, and yet he asked her permission to enter. If she had not loved him before now, she would have been unable to resist him, just for that fact. And he still wished to use the window. Which was both discreet, and arousing. And he was coming to her tonight.

Susan gave a quiet cough to remind Constance of her continued presence.

She smiled up at the maid.

Susan smiled back. 'Have you decided to listen to your heart after all, your Grace?'

'It beats so loudly when I think of him that I have been unable to do otherwise.' She allowed the maid to help her into her morning dress. 'I think, Susan, that there is no hope for me. It is not wise of me to want Mr Smythe. It would be much better could I bring myself to feel this towards Lord Endsted. But my mind will not obey reason. When I think of Tony, the sun shines brighter, the air smells sweeter, and I feel as if I could fly, rather than walk.'

Susan nodded. 'You are in love.'

Constance looked back at her, sadly. 'I never meant to be. I never have been, before. And I am not sure, when it ends, that I will like it very much.'

'It will be worth it,' Susan assured her. 'For you will always remember this morning.'

That night, supper was barely cold when she called for Susan to ready her for bed. It was foolish of her, she supposed, for it was far too early to expect a visit. But he had given no indication of the time he would come. And when he did arrive, she did not wish to waste a moment of his company in preparation. Susan had laid out her best night rail, and she allowed it to be put on, only to toss the thing aside as soon as her maid had left the room. Then she crawled naked between the sheets.

It was almost midnight when, at last, he climbed in the window, silhouetted in the light from the street. She leaned on her elbow and watched him, admiring his movements. How strange that he should be able to climb in and out as easily as going through the front door. And how accustomed she'd become to his habits.

'Good evening.' She could see his grin in the darkness, when he saw her already in bed. 'I hope I am not disturbing you.'

'Not at all.' She stretched and let the sheet slip down her body so that he could see she was bare beneath the linen.

He caught his breath at the sight. 'Not disturbed'? Give me fifteen minutes and you shall be.' He slipped off his coat and tossed it over a chair. 'You received the deed?'

'Yes. Thank you.'

He undid his cravat and tossed it and his shirt after the coat. 'Did you send your maid away this evening so that we might not be interrupted?'

'Yes,' she breathed. He was slim, unlike her husband. His belly was flat and his shoulders broad and she could watch the muscles move under the skin as he undressed.

He sat on the end of the bed and pried off his boots.

'I hope that she is on the other side of the house.' He looked over his shoulder at her. 'You were quite vocal last night. It is most gratifying to get such an enthusiastic response.'

She blushed. 'It was very... I don't think I... Thank you.'

He turned to look at her with a fond smile. 'You're very welcome.' He sighed and shook his head in amazement. 'And very, very beautiful. Especially as you are now, naked in bed, and waiting for me.' He stood and unfastened his breeches and let them drop to the floor. He was large, and already growing hard. But then, his whole body was well muscled and firm, and she longed to touch every inch of it. He stretched out on the bed beside her, with only the sheet separating their bodies.

He took her in his arms and cradled her against his body, and she felt the hair of his chest rubbing against her breasts and bringing every nerve alive in her.

In response, she kissed him.

There was nothing gentle in his answer as he kissed her back. There was the same intensity that she felt whenever he looked at her, as though he wanted to steal her away and keep her all to himself. His hands were on her back, stroking her and gripping her shoulders and her waist and anything he could reach.

She pushed the sheet down and out of the way so that she could feel even more of him.

And he pulled it back up to her waist, keeping them apart, but gripping her bottom and her legs so that she could feel how hard he was, even through the fabric.

She wrapped her legs around him, tangling in the sheet and rocking, letting the linen rub against them, as he reached to play with her breasts, cupping them with his hands, stroking and pulling at the nipples. And then he caught one of her hands, bringing it to his mouth to suck on the fingers and kiss the knuckles and the palm. At last, he whispered, 'If you would be so kind.' Then he led it down his body, over his chest and stomach, until it rested between his legs under the sheet.

She understood what he wanted, for she had often had to help her husband, before he was able to perform. But Anthony was not in obvious need of help. He was long and hard and ready, and he sucked in his breath when her hand touched him, and gritted his teeth in a smile.

She stroked him, running her hand along the smooth flesh and tightening around it, and he trembled next to her. She kissed his lips and bit his throat, and worked her way down his chest to explore his nipples with her tongue, tasting salt and feeling his gasps as her grasp grew stronger and longer and faster. She ran her other hand over his body, feeling the muscles tighten and his back arch as he grew near to climax and her own body grew wet and heavy, and eager to know his first thrust inside of her.

And when she knew it could not be much longer,

she reached to pull the sheet out of the way so that they could join. But he held fast to it.

Did he mean to come without her, as she had without him the night before? She had thought, the way he looked at her, that he had wanted more from her than this. Was it the woman he said he loved that kept him from completing the act with her? Her stroke faltered.

'Tony?'

'Just a moment, darling.' His words came between groans. 'Just a little while longer.'

'I must ask—'

'After, please. Anything.'

'But I need to know—'

'Constance, I am dying,' he begged. 'Finish what you have started.'

She stilled her hand, holding him in a loose grip, and said, 'Is there some reason that you cannot crawl beneath the sheet and finish yourself?'

He said through gritted teeth, 'I thought that would be obvious. I do not want to get you with child.'

She yanked her hand from his body and rolled away, turning her back to him and wrapping herself in the bed linens. 'Get out.'

He laid a gentle hand on her shoulder, and his voice was unsteady. 'I am sorry to be so selfish. You have needs as well and I should think of my lady before myself. But I have been able to think of nothing but your hand on me for the whole day...'

She shivered in the bed and wrapped the sheet even tighter around herself. 'I can see to my own needs from now on.'

'Constance,' he whispered. 'What is the matter?'

When she tried to speak, it felt as though her throat were full of tears. 'You know what is the matter. How could you say that? I trusted you. And how could you hurt me so? To use such an excuse to avoid making love, when you must know as well as the rest of the world that I have been barren for thirty years. Producing a child will not be at issue. If you have a distaste for me, or for the act, or if there is another woman, can you at least tell me the truth? Do you think me a fool?'

'Constance.' He pulled her to him, so that she could feel him, still hard, and pressing against her from behind. Then he rested his head against her shoulder, so that he might speak in her ear. 'I do not think you foolish. But I think that you have been told for so long that there is a deficiency in you that you believe it yourself. Now, answer me honestly. Have you ever lain with a man, other than your husband?'

'No, of course not. How could you say such a thing?'

'How old was he when you married?'

'He was almost two score.'

'And you were just out of the schoolroom, were you not?'

'Well, yes.'

'And did he have mistresses?'

She never liked to think of such things. But there had been the scent of strange perfume, and the occasional trace of rouge on his cravat, although she wore none.

'Constance?'

'Yes. There were other women.'

'But no rumours of bastards?'

'No.' The thoughts that she had never dared think, when Robert was alive, mingled with the doubts.

'Did you ever have to dismiss a chambermaid for getting herself in trouble? And I do not mean for carelessness with the silver.'

'No.'

'So your husband had no children when he married you, and in the last fifteen years he lay with several women, without issue. While you were only with him.' He placed a hand negligently on her hip. 'I told you before, Constance, I am not prone to gambling. But I'll wager, if we are careless and lower this sheet, you are liable to find that the problem was not yours, much to your regret.'

Regret? He must be mad. Awareness flooded her. Tony was young and strong and hard. Virile. And he wanted her, as much as she wanted him. If there was a chance, even the slightest chance, that she could ever hold a babe… She yanked the sheet out of his hand and turned to face him, wrapping her legs around his body so that his sex could rest against her.

She kissed him, and rubbed her body against his, urging him to do what she knew he wanted to.

And he muttered, 'You are not thinking clearly, Constance. God knows, I can hardly think at all. Now give me back the sheet before I do something that we may rue later.' But he did not push her away.

'Take me, Tony,' she murmured. 'I do not care. Take me, now.' And she reached between them to guide him into her body.

He took a long breath and stayed her hand. 'I must be mad to stop you. A moment. Please.'

There was a pause as he tried to remember what it was he wanted to say. 'You may not care now. But no child of mine shall be a bastard. If I am right and there is a consequence to this act, do you swear to me that you will tell me, and accept the next time I offer for you?'

'Yes,' she whispered. 'Now, do it.'

Still he waited, and he was trembling with the effort. 'There will be no fuss from you about my low birth, or my chosen profession, no nonsense about not knowing my family or my past. You will marry me without question, and follow where I lead.'

'Yes, Tony,' she panted. 'Yes, now just do it, before it is too late.'

And he rolled over her, thrust into her, shuddered and collapsed.

She held him close and smiled into his shoulder, at the feel of him filling her, the thought of his seed inside her, and the idea that she might not be dead inside after all.

He raised himself up on his arms to look down into her eyes. 'Woman, you are mad to be smiling at me. That was a pathetic effort on my part. I had hoped for so much more from our first true meeting. To leave you satisfied at least. But to so totally lose control of myself...'

'It was fine,' she assured him. 'I am just so glad that we were not too late.'

'Too late for what, sweet?'

'You almost did it without being within me. I had hoped that it would happen this evening. And it would be a shame if I had missed it.'

He was staring at her in a most unusual way. And he muttered, 'You husband was quite a bit older than you. Well, I suppose...'

And then he moved against her, to stroke inside her. 'I think, my darling, that if you thought that was to be an isolated incident, there is yet more to teach you.'

She gasped as he grew hard again and her body tightened in surprise.

He sucked in his breath. 'Do that again, love. Yes, just like that. And again. You are heaven, for I never expected to feel something so good in this life. You did not think I would stop at once, if you let me have you. I am insulted.'

More than once. He was right, there were things she

needed to learn. He was large and he was hard for her again. Her excitement grew at the thought.

He paused. 'Let us try something new.'

She wanted to argue that it was already new to her and quite good enough, when he had rolled so that she was lying on top of him.

She froze in confusion, wondering what he wished her to do next. And she shifted up on to her elbows so she could look at him. And the feeling took her. And she shifted, again. And again. And then she drew her legs up under her, and he grabbed her by the waist and let her do as she would, whispering words of encouragement as she rocked herself to climax upon him. Then he steadied her hips and thrust upward, again and again before his back arched, and he called her name, and then he pulled her down to lie on top of him again.

Their bodies were sweat slicked and chill in the darkness, and she shivered.

He threw the sheet over her back and wrapped his arms around her.

'You were right,' she whispered. 'That was even better.'

'And that was just the beginning,' he promised. 'We can try again, if you let me rest for a few minutes.'

'Minutes?' she asked in surprise.

'Or longer, if you wish.' He paused. 'I had rather hoped to stay the night, if you would allow it. I will be gone before dawn, of course. No one will see me.' He paused again, as though he thought, after what had happened, that she still might have the strength to deny him.

She snuggled into him, turned her face into his shoulder and kissed it. 'Stay as long as you wish.' Then she remembered her fears of the previous night. 'As long as it is safe for you to do so. Barton is not still searching for you, is he?'

'We are both safe from Barton. For a time, at least. He is not stalking me at the moment, and I hope he will have the sense to leave off bothering you, after the beating I gave him.' His arm wrapped protectively around her to pull her closer. 'So we should have several days of peace before Barton feels brave enough to try again. And I mean to spend every moment I can in your arms.'

Chapter Fifteen

Several days later, Tony was up early when Patrick brought him his breakfast tea, his pick working the lock mechanism in his practice safe. Barton's lock would be keyed differently, but it would be good to have the confidence that picking the first lock might give him, and some idea of the total amount of time involved.

And the time it had taken so far was considerable. He had been working on his own lock for several days without success, even though he could work unhindered and get hints from the shape of the key. Stanton was becoming restless. There had been a terse note, reminding Tony of the urgency of the situation, as if he did not know it himself. Much more time and the government would be forced to take action, and the rest of the story would play out in *The Times*, much to the embarrassment of all concerned.

Patrick cleared his throat to announce breakfast.

'Set the cup on the desk, Patrick.'

Patrick was looking over his shoulder.

'You may go.'

'I wouldn't dream of it. This is too interesting to miss.'

'That is my repayment for rescuing you from certain hanging so many years ago. Continued insolence. I had been better off to hire a servant in the ordinary way, than to take a charity case from Newgate.'

'And what would you have learned from this imaginary servant—how to polish your own boots? Have you tried oiling the lock?'

'And it has done me no good, other than to make the pick slip.'

'You could drill the lock out, and gain entry that way.'

'If I wished to announce the theft. I assume that Stanton wanted this done discreetly. And it would take even more time to drill through the steel.'

'Last night, were you attempting this at Barton's home? What methods did you employ? Did he leave you to work in peace, the whole night? For you were gone until almost dawn.'

Tony winced. He had gone to Barton's home and observed the study window for a time, but, seeing light and movement in the room, he had given it up as a bad job. 'He and I have come to an impasse, I fear. I have frightened him enough to keep him away from Constance. But now he will not leave his house, for fear of giving me a chance to enter. It is actually rather annoying, since it will make it difficult for me to finish the job, even if I can manage to open the safe.'

'If you were not with Barton, then where have you been spending your time?'

Tony cleared his throat. 'I spent the evening with the duchess.'

Behind him, Patrick chuckled. 'You have had better luck unlocking her affections than you have had with Barton's safe.'

Tony laid his check against the cool metal of the safe door and grinned. He had meant to visit her briefly the previous evening, and then return to his work. But several hours later, he was too exhausted to rise in any way, begging the woman to leave off tormenting him, assuring her that he had not an ounce of strength left in his body for the things she was suggesting.

And she had smiled at him, and rung for a bottle of champagne.

She had ignored him as he had argued that the wine would do more damage than good. Then she had taken the glass from his hand and drunk deeply. And she'd kissed her way down his body, taking little sips of the wine, and he'd had the strange sensation of bubbles on his skin, along with the kisses.

Then she had disappeared beneath the covers. And suddenly he was not nearly so exhausted as he had been moments before, and any plan he'd had of returning to Barton's was long forgotten.

He could hear the clink of the china as Patrick picked up the teacup and began to drink it himself. He glanced over his shoulder. His valet was balancing his hip on the corner of his master's desk, and helping himself to a scone to go with his tea. He glared.

Patrick shrugged. 'The tea is getting cold, and you would only get butter on your hands if you had a scone. I will get you more, when you have opened the lock. So, tell me, does the dowager have a lady's maid?'

'Don't be an idiot. Of course she does. And stop eating my breakfast.'

'Tell me about her.'

'I have been telling you about her for years.' Although he couldn't help but smile at the memory.

'Not the duchess. The maid.'

'She is just an ordinary maid. Not much in evidence, when I am there. Constance generally sends her to bed.'

'The dowager is a most understanding and generous mistress, to be sure. I look forward to meeting her, again. And her maid, as well. Whose name is?'

'Susan,' Tony responded.

'And I suppose she is old, pinch-faced, and sour tempered.'

'She appears to me to be a most pleasant girl of twenty, blonde, somewhat plump and quite attractive.'

Patrick offered a toast with his teacup. 'To the fair Susan. Now that things are settled, and the duchess knows who you are, I can hope but to spend a happy future, below stairs with a beautiful blonde.'

Tony swallowed and renewed his efforts with the lock. 'Well. About that…'

'You haven't told her. Have you?'

'We have been rather busy.'

Patrick poured another cup of tea. 'In the past week, you have spent more time in her company than you have in all of the previous thirty years.'

'But I would have to have been a fool to have spent it talking, Patrick. Apparently, the late duke was neglectful of his marital duties. And the duchess wishes to make up for lost time. I am happy to oblige, although I am near to exhaustion. Once the novelty of my visits wears off, we will have time to chat about old times. But until that time… Well, I'll be damned.'

The locked turned under his hand, and the door to the safe swung open.

'I have done it.' He stared from the lock to Patrick and back to the lock. 'I have picked a Bramah.'

Patrick stared over his shoulder at the open safe, and patted him on the back. 'Well done, sir. Do you mean to try the challenge lock in the Bramah Company window, next? You could claim the two hundred guineas.'

Tony sat on the edge of the desk. 'I cannot very well tell them it has been done. They'll want to know how I managed it. And then they will change the lock to make it impossible again.' He reached forward to touch the open door, as though he expected it to be an illusion. 'And worse yet, they'll wonder why a gentleman, who is not a locksmith by trade or by hobby, had reason to try.' He laughed to himself. 'I am the man that beat Bramah. But I cannot tell anyone, or I will not be able to use what I have learned.'

Patrick nodded in sympathy. 'But you can use the information now, can't you? Against Barton?'

Tony stared at the open safe. 'I certainly hope so. If the man ever leaves his house, I mean to try.'

Tony leaned against the trunk of the tree that had become his evening home. He had spent three nights, perched like a bird in front of Barton's house, watching the man sit in his study until almost midnight, only to be replaced by a servant, who was left to sleep in the chair by the desk. Tony had returned to Constance's rooms each night, and let her soothe the frustration away, only to see the process repeated again the next night.

Barton must know he was watching. The guard upon the things was obvious enough, and all carried out in plain view of the window. So it was left to him to find a way to force Barton from cover, or the pattern could play out indefinitely.

Tony glanced back at the house, in frustration. To

be so close to the plates, and finally in a position to have another go at the lock, only to be thwarted…

The room was empty.

He stared again. The lights were on, and the room was empty. He shifted his position in the tree to view it from another angle. There was no sign of life in the study.

His pulse quickened.

The front door of the house opened, and Barton appeared on the front step and paused, almost dramatically. He looked in the direction of Tony's tree and made a grand, welcoming gesture towards the house, before signalling to a servant to bring the carriage around.

Tony sat perfectly still, straddling his branch as the carriage accepted its owner and drove away. The bastard had known he was there, and known his location as well. And he was leaving the house in plain sight and daring Tony to enter.

It was a trap, of course. But an irresistible one. Barton knew, and was taunting him.

Tony considered. If he was wise rather than clever, he would head away from the danger, and not towards. But he was tired of sitting in trees and trying to wait the man out. Now or never, then.

He dropped to the ground and made his way stealthily across the grounds to the ornamental drainpipe at the corner of the house that had served as ladder on his last entry. He rattled it, examining the areas nearest the ground for loosened bolts. It seemed secure, and so he began his ascent, working up the first flight, and the next, to the level of the window he sought.

Only to slip rapidly down. He'd dropped almost ten feet, and very nearly lost his grip before regaining his hold.

The bastard had greased the metal. Tony grinned through gritted teeth. If he had been careless, other than merely rash, he might have fallen, as Barton had intended.

He examined the stone front of the house. A more difficult climb, but not impossible. Clinging to the pipe with his legs, he pulled gloves from his pockets to cover the grease on his hands. Then he renewed his grip and reached out with a leg, finding a toe-hold in the stone of the house. And then a hand hold. And so began his ascent again.

It was unlikely that Barton would guess his route and lay another trap, but Tony felt carefully as he went for loosened stones or chiselled mortar. He was progressing nicely, within an arm's length of the ledge beneath the window. He reached, grasped, and felt the pain before his fingers had fully closed on the bricks. When he pulled his hand away it was followed by a shower of broken glass.

He shook his hand to dislodge the shard that had poked through the palm of his glove, thanking God that the leather had taken the majority of the damage, and then reached out to brush the area clear, so that he might proceed.

An excellent effort, Barton. But not quite good enough. He examined the window for traps before opening it. It was mercifully clear and unlatched. Perhaps the next snare waited inside, since Barton did not think the window worthy of his effort. Tony made a quick circuit of the lit room before setting to work on the safe. No servants concealed behind furniture or curtains. And the key had been left on the inside of the door, as though he were invited to lock it, if he wished to work in privacy.

He turned the key in the door, and, as an afterthought, pushed a chair under the door handle as an additional safeguard. Then he set to work on the safe.

Tony tried to ignore the creeping flesh at the back of his neck. There was something wrong. He had expected the traps. But there should have been more of them. Aside from the unpickable nature of the lock, which was proceeding rather nicely, he thought. There had to be something that Barton knew, that he did not. The man would not relinquish the prize so easily, if he thought Tony could make it into the room. There must be something he was not considering, then. The thought nagged at him, as he shifted the pick in his hand to catch the next slider. Barton could not have concealed the plates on his person before leaving. They were not huge, but too large to slip into a coat pocket.

He would not leave something so precious unguarded, would he?

And then the thought hit him. Barton might leave the plates unguarded to go to something he wanted more.

Tony had left Constance. Unprotected.

Even as he thought it, he felt the pick slip home to move the last slider. With a slight turn of his wrist, he opened the lock and the door to the safe swung wide.

He reached into the opening.

There were no plates within.

Chapter Sixteen

Constance was waiting in her sitting room until it was late enough to go to bed. Her life was falling into a familiar pattern, now that Tony was part of it. She would nap in the afternoon, and have dinner, alone. She then sent the servants to bed early and spent the rest of the evening reading before the fire until almost midnight. Then she would find her own way to her room.

Shortly afterwards, her lover would come, and they would pass the hours until dawn.

Tonight, she had chosen Byron to keep her company until bedtime. She smiled and closed her eyes. When she had asked Tony to read to her, he had looked into her eyes and recited the poems from memory.

If she was not careful, she would become quite spoiled by his attentions. When the time came to return to reality, she would remember that Tony's behaviour was an aberration of character, and a sign of the minimal depth of their relationship. Men might spout poetry to their mistresses, but never to their wives.

But it was lovely, all the same. 'So lovely,' she whispered.

'Yes, you are.' When she opened her eyes, Jack Barton was standing in the doorway.

She stood up and backed away, until she felt her shoulders bump the wall behind her. 'How did you get into my home?'

He smiled at her, as always. 'You gave me your key.'

'Only because you forced me to. And Tony got it back for me.'

'Tony.' Barton sniffed in dismissal. 'He is not much of a thief if he does not realise that keys can be copied. I let him take the one, and kept the duplicate, assuming rightly that I might need it later.'

'Get out. I shall ring for the servants.'

'I would not advise that.' Barton pulled a pistol from his pocket, and pointed it in her direction.

'Go ahead and shoot. You would not dare,' she said and started for the bell pull.

'Not you,' he replied. 'But I will shoot the first one through the door, if you ring for help. If you remember my last visit, you know I am capable of it.'

Her hand faltered before it reached the pull.

Barton nodded. 'Very good. You must agree, it is better if we remain alone. And since you have dismissed the staff for the evening, they will not disturb us.'

'But we will not be alone for long,' she threatened. 'I am expecting a guest.'

'Anthony Smythe?' Barton shook his head in disappointment. 'I doubt he will be troubling us again. It was very simple, in the end, to beat your lover. It is a pity that I could not be there to see him fail. But I needed to be away from the house, to lure him in.'

'What do you mean?' Constance felt a chill.

'The minute I was away, I have no doubt that he rushed into the house, ready to search the study. If he made it past the traps I set for him without falling to his death, he is still in for a nasty shock. The safe he has been trying to open for the last several weeks is, to the best of my knowledge, empty. I have never had reason or ability to open it. It was left by the previous owner of the house. For all I know, the man took the key to the grave with him. If he has not found them already, I doubt that your Mr Smythe will have sense to intuit the location of the things he is looking for.

'I fear, darling, that in his initial excitement, he may have forgotten all about you.'

Constance tried not to imagine Tony, dangling unsteadily from a ledge or lying in a broken heap at the base of Barton's house. He had made it into the house. She must believe that he had survived, if she meant to keep her wits about her. 'I doubt he is so easy to beat

as all that. He will come to my aid when he realises
that you have tricked him.'

'But if your vulnerability occurs to him later, he
will come rushing back here, breakneck, to rescue
you. He enters your room through the window, does
he not?'

She stared at him, keeping her expression a blank.

'Oh, come now. There are no secrets left between
us. I have seen the ivy that leads right to your room. I
doubt an agile climber could resist such an easy path.
Now, where was I?

'I have left him my plans for the evening. When he
realises that I mean to have you while he is chasing after
nothing, he will come rushing back to this house, to the
bedroom, where he expects to find us. I will be waiting…' he gestured with the pistol in his hand '…to rescue you from the intruder, bent on entering your room.
One shot, as he is framed in the window. He will die
from the bullet, or the fall, or a combination of the two.'

'It will be murder. And I will tell anyone who will
listen.'

'I doubt anyone will, Constance. And even if they
do, you might think before you speak. We will be in
your room, together. There will be no question as to
why I am there. It would be better, for you, should the
world think that Smythe was attempting to rob you. If
it appears you were entertaining two gentlemen, you
will be the talk of the town.'

The book of poems slipped from her hands and dropped to the floor.

'And you will want me to be free of prosecution. You will need my protection for quite some time, I think. If I am in jail for murder, or worse, you will gain nothing by it but revenge. Your reputation will be in tatters. You will not see another penny out of your idiot nephew, for he will cut you from the family for the disgrace.

'On the other hand, if I am free, I will take care of you, just as I have always promised. We may have to leave the country, at least for a time. My business is not going quite so well as I'd hoped. But we will have the comfort of each other.'

Constance felt something snap, deep inside her. This was not how her life was to end. She was not some pawn to be passed from man to man and abandoned as they chose. She could not very well sit waiting for a rescue that might never come. Suppose Tony was dead, as Barton hoped. Or worse yet, on his way to her window so that she could watch him shot before her eyes and disgraced as a burglar.

She would not let it happen. If anyone was to be shot tonight, it would not be Tony.

Barton gestured with the gun.

'We will go to your room, and wait.'

'I suppose I have no choice,' she said.

'We have been over this before, Constance.'

'If I submit willingly to you, will you spare Anthony Smythe?'

Barton laughed. 'That offer is no longer available to you. What transpires now is a matter between gentlemen. You need not concern yourself with it.'

'It is not the act of a gentleman to shoot an unsuspecting man.'

He smiled. 'It is plain, Constance, that you are trying to prolong the inevitable. You have no need to be nervous, you know. I have every intention of being a gentle and courteous lover. Fine things should be savoured, not devoured.'

There he went again, referring to her as a thing. Not for very much longer, she hoped. Any minute, Tony would be here to put a stop to it.

Or he would not, and she would have to act for herself.

Barton reached across the table to stroke her hand. 'And you are fine indeed. Your skin is soft, your eyes are bright…'

Her teeth were good, and her coat glossy. Soon he would be extolling her good wind and her ability to take jumps at the gallop. Tony never wasted half so much time on pretty words. And yet she had no doubt that he found her beautiful. She felt the anger in her, rising to push out the fear.

'I will take great pleasure in loving you…'

And what was she to take from the experience? At

least Tony did not blather on about how much he would enjoy being with her, although he clearly did. He seemed most concerned with how she felt about it. This man was obsessed with bedding her, nearly insane with it.

'Come, let me show you.' He rose and offered her his hand, and gestured towards the door with his gun.

She looked at the hand held out to her. Tony might be dead already. And if that was true, there would be no last-minute rescue. But if he was dead, then it did not matter, one way or the other, what happened to her. She no longer cared, so there was nothing to be afraid of.

She looked at Barton. He had seemed so frightening, but he was a pathetic creature who could think no further than the bed in her room. She knew his weakness, and she could exploit it to her advantage.

'Very well.' She took his hand and he escorted her towards the stairs, a pace behind, with the gun in his pocket. She turned as they were halfway up. 'And you intend to be gentle?'

'Of course.'

She allowed a small disappointed sigh to escape her lips.

Behind her, on the steps, she heard the slight hesitation in his step.

She paused again. 'Robert was always very careful, when we were together. I assumed that it was the fault of age. Tony, as well, treated me as though I were made of glass.' She turned to look back at Barton. 'Some day, perhaps I will find someone who is not afraid to give me what I want.' She glanced back at him and saw the avaricious glimmer in his eyes.

'You do not wish me to be gentle?'

'Let me be plain, Jack. You are a cold-blooded brute and I detest you. But perhaps I have had my fill of gentleman lovers. You mean to have me and I cannot stop you. But if you must, then do not bore me with talk of gentleness.' She turned back to him on the stairs and kissed him, biting his lip.

She heard the intake of breath as she released him and watched his eyes go dark. He hurried the last few steps to draw even with her, pushing her back against the wall to kiss her hard in return.

She moaned convincingly back at him, tangling her hand in his hair and running a hand down his spine.

He pulled away again, smiling at her in surprise. And then his gaze turned suspicious. 'If this is a trick, I will make you pay for it.' But she could see in his eyes that he wanted to believe her.

'You mean to make me pay, no matter what, Jack. There is nothing left to threaten me with.' She walked the last few steps to her room, stepped inside and closed the door behind them.

He was on her as soon as the door was shut, shoving her against the wall, his fist in her hair and his mouth on hers. She felt his hands gripping her shoulders and fumbling at the front of her gown for her breasts.

Neither hand held the gun.

She made as if to hold him about the waist, then plunged her hand into his pocket to seize the pistol and point it into his ribs.

It took a moment for him to recognise the feel of the metal barrel in his stomach, and stop molesting her. 'Constance!'

'Step away from me, Jack. And do not make any sudden movements. I do not know much of guns, but I seriously doubt that I will miss you, should I shoot.'

'Yes, Jack. Do step away from her. For if she does not want to shoot you, I most assuredly do.'

Tony's voice startled her so much that she almost dropped the gun.

Seeing her indecision, Barton made a lunge for the weapon only to come up short, as Tony grabbed him by the coat collar and yanked him away from her, and back into the room. Barton tripped and landed hard on the floor, momentarily dazed.

'Constance, if you don't mind?' Tony held out a hand for the gun, and she gingerly handed it to him.

He pointed it at Barton, and confided, 'I really don't know much more about weapons than you do, but I should hate to see you kill him, no matter how much he might deserve it. If either of us must shoot, let it be me.'

'You're all right,' she breathed, leaning back to let the wall support her weight.

He reached over and yanked hard on the bell pull to summon the servants, and glanced apologetically at Constance, before focusing again on Barton. 'I fear, darling, that I cannot keep my presence here a secret. I will need help removing this refuse from your room.

'You will never believe the night I've had. First a greased drainpipe. Then a handful of broken glass. And when at last I get the damn safe open, there is no sign of the plates.' He shook his finger at Barton.

'You thought you had me there, I'll wager. And perhaps, if you were decent to your servants, they'd have bothered to clear the evidence of the true hiding place out of the grate.' He pulled a burned scrap of paper from his pocket, and held it out for Barton to see. 'You burned a book, didn't you? Two, actually. Volumes one and two of *A History of British Currency.*'

He glanced at Constance again. 'That is Jack's idea of wit, darling. Let us be glad you will not have to suffer with it. He ripped the books from their bindings and burned them, then wrapped the plates in the book covers and put them back on the shelves. I have spent countless hours, fiddling with picks to crack that safe, and all for no reason. The plates were in plain sight and I could have left with them at any time.'

There was a sharp knocking at the door and Constance rushed to let the servants enter. Susan entered, in her night clothes, accompanied by…

Constance stared in shock. Tony's valet, Patrick, hair mussed and in his shirtsleeves, had followed her maid into her bedroom.

Even Tony looked surprised.

Patrick shrugged. 'I recognised the pull on the bell rope. You ring as if you are trying to yank it off the wall. Most distinctive, sir.'

'And you happened to be here, by fortunate coincidence?' Tony enquired.

'With you spending so many evenings from home, I had little to occupy my time. And it occurred to me that there might be another who would sympathise with my idleness.'

Susan giggled.

Tony struggled to find an appropriate response, before giving up. 'Well, you will not be idle tonight.' He pointed to Barton on the floor. 'Patrick, I wish this removed. From the room, certainly. From the country, if possible. I understand there are often ships in need of crew and none too particular about where the men come from. Use your initiative.'

Patrick looked at Barton, and back to the maid beside him. And he said softly, to Susan, 'This is the man who hurt you?'

Susan's eyes grew round, and she nodded her head.

Patrick's smile was broad and full of menace. Suddenly, he did not look like a humble manservant, but a large, and very threatening, man. He seized Barton from off the floor and punched him once, hard and in the face. 'No problem, sir.' He dragged the limp body towards the door.

'Breakfast will be late tomorrow, Patrick,' Tony called after him. 'Do not trouble yourself.'

'Very good, sir.'

Susan stepped out of the way and closed the door again.

Tony listened to the sound of Patrick and Barton retreating down the hall, before stepping close and seizing her around the waist. Then he spun her around in his arms, kissed her once, full on the mouth, and threw her on to the bed.

He was alive. Young and strong and safe. And she loved the feel of his hands on her, even as her mind struggled to sort out what had just happened. She pulled herself up to lean upon her elbows, trying to regain decorum. 'Tony, what the devil are you doing?'

He was standing over her with a most curious expression on his face, a mixture of joy and lust. 'Celebrating. You are safe, and Barton is in the soup. And I have done it, Constance. I have picked the unpickable Bramah lock. What say you to that?'

'Thank you?' she said, hesitantly.

'Actions speak louder than words, Constance.' And he climbed into bed after her and threw up her skirts.

'You do not mean…' She reached to smooth her skirts back down.

'Oh, yes, I most certainly do.' He caught her hand, and placed it on the front of his breeches, so she could feel how ready he was. Then he began to undo his buttons.

She had just threatened to shoot a man, after attempting to seduce him, and now, she was going to make passionate love to another. If she looked into the mirror, would she recognise the woman she saw? 'Do not be ridiculous. I cannot. I am still dressed. The door is not locked. I—'

He pushed her down on to the bed, kissing her in a way that left no doubts as to how much he wanted her, and how soon.

'Well, at least take off your boots,' she suggested breathlessly, recognising the old familiar Constance, trying to regain control.

He ignored her.

And the woman that she had become did not care in the slightest. He came into her fast and hard, and she arched as the shock of it ran through every nerve in her body and hummed in her blood. And as he thrust, he told her of things he wanted to do to her, and with her, and for her, each one more scandalous than the last.

And she wanted it all. She wanted his breath on her throat and his voice in her ear, and his body hard inside her for ever. But for now, she wanted him harder and faster, and she told him so over and over again until her breath was a gasp and her voice a sob and her body was trembling with the need for release. And when he demanded it, she came with him, and they collapsed, shaking with weakness, into a tangle on the bed.

He moved against her and she caught her breath in surprise as her body shuddered again, and he rolled away so that he could look into her eyes, reached a hand to her and stroked her to another climax.

And somewhere, deep down, her brain was screaming that this was madness, and it must stop. What had she just promised him? And what could he make her do, when he took her to this state? He knew her body, and he used his knowledge. She was helpless to resist him because it was all too good, and the waves ran through her again as she trembled at his touch.

She looked into his eyes. They were not empty, like Barton's, but full of shadows. He looked into her soul and he knew her. But who was he?

She sat up and looked around her in confusion. She was lying fully dressed in her bed with a strange man, whose boots were leaving mud on the sheets. And he'd just taken her so violently that her body ached, and then soothed the ache away with his hand.

And he'd done it all because she begged him to.

Now, he was undressing her with exquisite care, undoing her gown and removing her stays, pausing to touch and kiss with featherlightness in ways that he knew pleased her. And now he was taking the pins from her hair and letting it down, combing it out with his fingers.

He knew every inch of her. He knew her life and her finances, and her body, all the intimidate details that she'd never dared share with Robert...

Why had she told him? And why had she not told her husband? Who had she become, now that she'd chosen to fall from virtue with such wanton abandon? Because she certainly was no longer herself.

And who was he? What did she know of him, other than that he was a thief, and that he said she could trust him?

And that he loved another.

He was still fully dressed, and she was naked beside him with her hair free around her shoulders. He was smiling his enigmatic smile as he admired her in her vulnerability.

She pulled the sheet around herself before she let him pull her down beside him and love her again.

He looked at her curiously, waiting for her to speak.

'It is truly over, then, with Barton?'

'He would be a fool to remain in the country, even if Patrick allows him to. I will turn the plates over to the Earl of Stanton in the morning, to be destroyed. If Barton reappears, St John will have no trouble hanging him as a traitor. You need never worry about him again.'

He might as well have been speaking nonsense.

'You spoke of the plates before. What are they? And what does St John Radwell have to do with it all?'

Tony pulled away from her, and puzzled for a moment, before saying, 'Ah. Yes. I'd meant to tell you about that. Barton was a counterfeiter. Or wished to be. And St John works for the government, and they wanted the plates back, so he hired me to steal them.'

'So you are not a thief at all.'

'Well, I am still a thief. A very good one. But currently, I steal when I am ordered to, by a higher authority.' He grinned. 'Perhaps I am a humble civil servant. I quite like the idea. It sounds most respectable.'

'Then why did you not tell me?'

He looked evasive. 'Frankly, it had not really occurred to me that there would be a difference. Stealing is stealing, and I have not much concerned myself with the reason. St John does not wish me to discuss our association, since the world knows little of what he does, and to reveal my part in it reveals his.'

'So you are a spy, then.'

He thought about it. 'I suppose you could say that.'

The truth began to dawn on her. 'When I found you here, in this room, you were spying on me. And my best friend's husband sent you. Because he thought I was a traitor. Just like Barton.'

Tony tried to laugh, but it came out sounding small and nervous. 'I soon set him straight on that. The very first night, I told him you were innocent.'

It was some consolation, she supposed, to know that he thought she was innocent, even though he continued to spy upon her. 'And this great secret, which you could not share with me to spare my feelings. Is that the only secret? Or are there other things that you have not told me?'

He looked positively uncomfortable, and had trouble meeting her gaze. 'Well, everyone has secrets, I suppose.'

'But you have more than most, I think. What is it that you are still not telling me, that makes you so evasive now?'

He attempted to laugh again, and failed completely. 'You make it sound very ominous. I swear, I was not attempting to hide things from you.'

'But you have hidden them all the same. I do not like being played for a fool, Tony. Not by my friends, and not by you.'

He flinched at the word 'friends' and then looked her squarely in the eyes. 'I do not think you a fool, nor do I wish to play games with you. But I wish, Constance, that by now you would have looked with your own eyes and known the truth for yourself.'

'So that you did not have to admit to it? What is it, that is so horrible that you cannot speak it out loud? You had the gall to offer me marriage, and yet you cannot manage to be honest with me.'

'Perhaps it is because I knew how you would respond, should I tell you the whole truth. It is quite plain, Constance, that whatever you might pretend, on the subject of love you are as cold hearted as any woman in my experience. It was a hundred times easier for me to steal your heart than it would have been to gain it by honest means. If I came to you and presented my case openly, with the rest of your suitors, you would have dismissed me as unworthy of your time and gone after Endsted and his title.' He was able to laugh again as he mocked her. 'But it excites you if I approach in darkness and you let me take what I want from you.'

Then he touched her skin, and her body responded with a shudder of passion. 'You want what I can give you,' he said, 'but you wish to be free of me when the sun rises, in case there is a better offer. And I let you use me, because, God help me, I cannot resist you.'

'I was using you, was I?' She looked down at her bare body, next to his. 'When you threw me down and took me, just now? Of course, you did manage to get rid of Barton for me. Although you said before that you did not wish to wait for payment, until after the deed was done, I should think, after tonight, that our accounts must be close to even.'

'And now you are trying to tell me that you behaved thus just so that I would help you?' He stared at her in disbelief. She could see the pain in his eyes. 'Why are you doing this, Constance?'

'I do what I must to survive, Tony. I did when I married Robert, and I must continue doing so, now he is gone. I am beautiful, or so everyone tells me. If that is all I bring to a marriage, then I must hold out for the best offer. Soon the beauty will fade, and, if I am not careful, I will be left with nothing.'

'Just as you were when your husband died?' His smile was sardonic. 'A pity. For he seemed such a good choice and it all came to naught.'

'Do not dare to question my marriage, you—'

'Thief? Criminal? Commoner?' He got out of the bed and did up his breeches. 'Guilty on all counts.' He turned and bowed to her, tugging his forelock. 'And now you no longer need my services, am I dismissed, your Grace?'

It was over. His business was completed, and he was leaving, unless she could think of a way to stop him. But she was not sure she wanted him to stay, if she could not trust him to tell her the truth. 'Well, you didn't think it would last for ever, did you?' She heard the quaver in her own voice, and wondered if she needed to speak the words to herself.

'No, actually, I didn't. In my experience, happiness seldom lasts for long. But I thought when we parted, you would not need to convince yourself that you had been coerced. Do you need me to be the villain of the piece? Does it make you feel better to think you had no choice?'

He stepped closer and she shrank from him, pulling the bedclothes up to cover her nakedness.

'Let me tell you the way I remember what happened. I came to your bed because you invited me there. You wanted *me*, your Grace, because you knew what I could do for you, and it had nothing to do with money or deeds. You wanted me to love you as your husband could not.'

Even as he said it, she could feel the need burning inside of her.

'Now you are going to pretend that while you writhed in ecstasy beneath me, it was because I was forcing you to make a noble sacrifice to preserve your reputation for someone more suitable.'

He reached to his throat and ripped off his cravat and threw it to the floor. Then, he opened his shirt and pointed. 'See there? These are the marks of your kisses on my throat. Your nails have raked my back and your hands have held me so tight that my arms are bruised. I've heard every word you've said to me, when we made love. I know what you felt.

'Perhaps there is already another player waiting in the wings. Someone with a title, or money honestly come by. Someone you can introduce to your friends.'

She watched as he stepped towards the door of her room, preparing to walk out, only to check himself, curse, and turn as usual to leave by the window. 'He can be the one to ruin your reputation. For I suspect the next man to share this bed will think nothing of arriving at night and leaving by the front door in the morning for all to see.'

He reached into his jacket and dropped a card on the floor. 'If you need further assistance, go directly to my man of business. There will be funds for you, should you ever need them. What I have is yours to command. You need never speak to me again, so there will be no misunderstanding of my motives. As I told you before, I do not expect payment for acts done in friendship. But do not ever claim again that you need do something against the wishes of your conscience, because of a lack of funds.'

And he walked across the room and stepped out of the window and out of her life.

Chapter Seventeen

Tony woke as the earth tipped out from under him, and he landed face first on the floor of the study.

'Rise and shine, Smythe.' Stanton's voice was disgustingly cheerful as he dropped the wing chair with a crash, next to Tony's prone body.

'What the devil… You bastard!' Light came streaming in the windows as his visitor yanked aside the velvet curtains. The sunlight was blinding, stabbing into his brain, as he tried to focus on the figure in silhouette against the morning sun.

'And a pleasant good morning to you, as well. You missed our regular appointment. Twice. To prevent your missing it a third time, I have come to you.' St John stared down at him in bemusement. 'I have seen better things than you stuck to the bottom of my boot after a night in Whitechapel. And smelled better as well. For God's sake, man, pull yourself together. There is work to be done.'

'I resign.'

'I am not totally sure that that would be permitted. While you have not technically enlisted, I might still find a way to court-martial you. Perhaps not. Thieves in the army are usually flogged or hanged. Do you have a preference?'

'Why don't you just shoot me and get it over with?'

'Very well, then.' And before Tony could process the action, St John produced a pistol and put a bullet into the wall next to him.

Tony rolled to the left, covering his head with his hands as the sound of the shot echoed in his ears. 'What the hell are you doing in my house, firing a weapon? Are you mad? The ball missed my head by inches. You could have killed me.'

St John righted the wing chair and sat in it, arms folded. 'The ball missed you by several feet, just as I intended. I am an excellent shot, especially at such close range. But I am pleased to see you have recovered the will to live.' He gestured to the wreckage of the room. 'And the ball in the woodwork is the least of the problems here. Explain this, please.'

Tony looked at the mess he had made of the room. The mirror was broken, and Patrick had not bothered to replace it. It was just as well, for he had a fair idea of what he must look like after who knew how long without a razor or change of linen. He did not need to see his reflection.

Broken glasses littered the cold fireplace, and empty bottles littered the floor. Patrick had continued to bring the bottles for a while, after refusing him glasses, and hiding the windows behind the curtains so as to remove temptation. And now he refused him brandy, hoping to starve him out. It had made Tony so angry that he'd thrown a small table at the head of his retreating servant.

And missed. He glanced at the chipped plaster of the wall and the pieces of broken table on the floor below it. 'When you came, did I still have a servant to let you in?'

'Yes. Patrick is most concerned about you. He sent me up alone and told me not to turn my back on you if there was anything left for you to throw. Now tell me, what happened to this room?'

'A woman,' Tony said with finality.

'On the contrary, my man, I think it was you who did it.'

'A woman happened to me, you idiot. And I happened to the room.'

'What a relief. I thought it might be serious. Get yourself a bath and a shave and another woman. And then get back to work.'

'There are no other women. None but her,' Tony said sourly.

St John sighed. 'May the good Lord spare me from melodrama. Are we all to suffer for your broken heart? Her Grace the Dowager Duchess of Wellford was miles above you, in case you hadn't noticed. I don't see why—'

'How did you know?' Tony demanded.

'Let me see.' St John tapped his chin. 'Perhaps it is because I am a spy, you moron. I set you to watch her. You were nervous when I suggested it. You have been distraught since the moment the project was completed. And you look like a gaffed flounder whenever I mention her name. As I was saying, the Dowager Duchess? I am most relieved to find that she had no part in any of this. She is a lovely girl. A favourite of my wife's. What I'd have told Esme if I'd had her friend arrested for treason, I cannot say. And they are both quite angry with me for my part in this, although I expect to find forgiveness in time.

'Tony…' his tone became quiet and sympathetic '…Constance is charming, pleasant and totally out of your league. Far be it from me to let the cold light of day into your tragic fancy. While you have enough money to support a wife and a brood of little Smythes in sufficient comfort, I would suggest you choose a woman who is not a renowned beauty, accustomed to a thirty-room mansion and a coronet. Unless you wish to spend the rest of your life tossing furniture against the walls of a darkened room.'

Tony sat on the floor, trying not to notice the shambles he'd made of his life. He'd held on to the dream for so long that it had seemed quite natural, when the moment came, to have Connie fall eagerly into his arms. He'd had no trouble believing what he'd wanted to believe, that there was much more to it than there actually had been. He'd been a glamorous diversion, and an answer to so many of her problems, that she had succumbed to temptation, only to regret it later.

Perhaps, if he had taken time to court her, instead of simply seducing her, she'd have taken the whole thing more seriously. Perhaps not. It was a bit late to un-ring that particular bell.

And now Stanton was staring at him, waiting for a response. If he did not think of her, or the last few weeks, or any of the foolish assumptions he'd had over the last thirteen years… If he could focus on the task immediately in front of him, he would be able to move forwards, and put some space between himself and the whole situation.

He pulled himself up to his feet, leaning on the corner of the mantel. He could feel the brandy still fogging his brain and muffling the sound of his last argument with Constance, as it echoed endlessly in his head. Perhaps, if he had something to do with his time and kept very busy, he could ignore it all together.

Perhaps he would fall off an ivy trellis or out of a window somewhere and never have to think of anything again. But he could not stay locked up in his rooms, alone with the knowledge that the dream that had sustained him for many lonely years was over.

He brushed imaginary dust from his stained shirt, and lifted a stubbled chin to his guest. 'Very well, then. I've made an ass of myself, and you have seen it. But the worst of it is over, I think. If you still wish to employ me, then give me time to bathe, shave and change. And then tell me what you want taken.'

St John smiled as if nothing unusual had occurred. 'Good man.'

'Susan, you know I don't take milk in my tea.'

Her maid looked at her with guilty eyes. 'I thought perhaps, your Grace, you might wish to try something more fortifying. Now that autumn is here, I mean. It wouldn't do to take a chill.'

'Fortifying.' She looked at the tea. It was wretched stuff, but Susan was right. It was probably more nourishing. She took a sip.

Susan added, 'If you are not feeling well, your Grace, there is a lady in Cheapside that sells certain herbs. And when brewed up in a tea, these tend to clear up the sort of malady that you might be coming down with.'

'No!' Her hand went instinctively to cover her belly. She relaxed. 'I am sorry, Susan. I did not mean to shout so. You were right the first time to put milk in my tea. No matter how I might complain, it is good for me. And perhaps an egg and a bit of dry toast. Could you bring it to my room? I do not feel like going downstairs until I am sure that I will not be sick.'

There was no point in pretending any more with Susan, who knew her cycle almost as well as she did herself. She was two months gone with child.

'Very good, your Grace. But...' Susan left the statement open. She dare not ask the question, but she wanted an answer, all the same. Something must be done. They must leave London and retire quietly to the country where she could have the babe in secret. Or she must take the herbs and end it.

'Please, Susan. A little breakfast, perhaps.'

'Very good, your Grace.'

Her maid left the room, and she turned to the window, staring out into the garden. The trellis below her was bare, and she could see that it had been as if she had installed a ladder to her bedroom window. The garden gate and wall were still an easy climb, although the garden had less cover than when it had been in full bloom.

She closed her eyes, trying to imagine him making his way across it. It wouldn't happen, of course. She had seen nothing of him for a month and a half. Even when she had gone out in public, the most she'd heard was someone mentioning that Anthony Smythe had just been in attendance, but had retired early. Or was expected, but seemed to be late.

He was avoiding her. And she could hardly blame him.

Fortunately, other men were not. Endsted had returned, and renewed his attentions with a kind of plodding respectability that rekindled her hopes for the future. And other, more eligible, men were more respectful, now that Barton was no longer warning off suitors and spreading rumours about her.

Of course, in a few short months, everyone would know that the rumours were true. If she wished to marry well, she needed to act quickly to put an end to the pregnancy. It was just as her own mother would have told her to do, had anything stood between her and her goal.

And it was the sensible thing to do, she reminded herself. She had proved her fertility to herself, at least. She could hint to any man who showed serious interest that she had reason to believe the problems getting an heir were her late husband's and not her own. She could find another peer, and resume her status in society. She could have her comfortable old life back. But this time she might have children, as well as a husband.

She wrapped her arms around her stomach. Or she could go to Tony, and never be content again. She would spend her life alternately terrified by his job, and frustrated by his carefree attitude about the risks and his unwillingness to share everything that was in his heart or his mind. She might never have his full heart, and perhaps some day he would leave her to chase the dream woman he longed for. But when he came to her at night, she would have his undivided attention.

And she would not have a family in the future. She would have the baby she'd always wanted. The one that was growing in her now would be warm in her arms in a few months, smiling up at her, with his father's smile. And no matter what might happen, she would love them both with her whole heart, for how could she help but do otherwise?

Susan returned with the tray, setting it gently down upon the bed.

'Thank you, Susan. I am sure that I will feel much better after a little breakfast. And I will not be wanting any herbs.' She looked at her maid. 'I have waited too long for this. No matter what, I will not end it.'

Susan looked at her with pity. The poor abandoned duchess and her bastard. How could she explain that it was only pride keeping her from doing what she had promised?

Pride and the whirlwind of emotions that caught at her, every time she looked at the future. She had thought it would be easier to send him away than to keep him close. But life without him was every bit as hard as life with him had been.

She had told him it was over, and she'd regretted it the moment the words had been out of her mouth. She had finally managed to make him angry. He had shouted so. And his words had been so bitter. It was not, as she had expected, the cavalier agreement that the time had come to part. She had cut him to the heart in one stroke.

She'd cut herself as well. She had stood, frozen, watching him go. Wanting to call him back, even as he stepped through the window.

Every night since, she'd thought of him, burning hot and cold, with desire, or remorse, or longing, or the strange sensations coursing through her body that she had come to know as pregnancy.

She was having his child. Even better, their child. She could no more end it than she would end her own life. To be able to have something so precious, a gift that he had not wanted to give her, for fear that it would ruin her. Even then, he'd cared more for her reputation than he did his own pleasure. He'd left a bit of himself behind for her to keep, after vowing that he would protect her, and the babe, if it came to that.

He had never said he loved her. But did she really need to hear the words, if he would behave thus?

How could she have been so blind? He might not love her with the grand passion she wished, but he cared for her in all the ways that mattered.

She loved him, with a dizzying, soul-wrenching intensity that was nothing like the warm glow she had felt for Robert. And doubted that she could bring herself to marry another, no matter what Tony might feel for her.

Constance reached beneath her pillow for the strip of linen, hidden there. A man's cravat, carefully folded, hidden where she could touch it, when the night was dark and she was feeling most alone. If she could bring herself to admit that she had been wrong, and persuade him to forgive her, she might never be alone again.

'Susan,' she called. 'Lay out my clothes. I am going out.'

Chapter Eighteen

Patrick announced her, and she entered the study more hesitantly than she had the last time she'd needed a favour from him. She was dressed differently as well. Where she had come to seduce before, today she was attired modestly: the low square neck of her bodice filled with a fichu, the skirt of the dress cut so that it revealed nothing of the changes already taking place in her body.

Tony was sitting at his desk, papers spread out in front of him, but he rose as she entered. She thought she detected a rush in the movements, as though he was caught off guard and took a moment to control his actions, before she noticed. 'Your Grace?'

He gestured her to the chair in front of the desk and then seated himself again. 'To what do I owe the pleasure?' There was no trace of irony in his voice. There was no emotion of any kind.

'Do I really need a reason to visit, after what we have known together?'

He looked at her. 'In a word, yes. It has taken me several weeks to recover from our last discussion, and I have no wish to be unnecessarily reminded of it.' He was staring at her body. 'Unless…'

'I have come to say that I am sorry.' She hung her head.

He looked at her with concern. 'Your Grace, you are white as a sheet. A drink, perhaps?' He turned to the decanter on the desk and his glass next to it, and sighed. He finished the contents in a gulp. Then he wiped the rim and poured her a small brandy.

She found it an oddly fastidious gesture, from one who had known her so intimately. She took the glass, sniffed at the brandy, and felt her stomach roll. She set it down untasted. 'I was wrong to leave you with the impression that I viewed your visits as unwelcome, or that I felt them to be a duty or an obligation, or anything that might be construed as a repayment of debt.'

'Thank you,' he said softly. 'That is something, at least.'

'It was just that, with the threats and the stress of the debts, and not knowing how to go on, I was not myself.'

His gaze was flat and sceptical.

'I am normally a most proper and respectable person,' she continued. 'Although you would not know it by my behaviour when alone with you. Had it not been for circumstances, I am sure I would never have behaved as shamelessly as I had, or as abominably as I did in ending it.'

He rose. 'And now you have quite undone any good you did before. If you wish to discount your behaviour with me as an aberration, then it is better we remain apart to avoid disappointment. If we are together again, either you will be horrified by your continued deviance, or I will be crushed by the lack of it. Please leave me, now. Unless…' he stared at her '…there is any other reason for you coming here.'

She was afraid to meet his gaze. 'There is another thing. I know that you made me promise to not trouble you on that account, but I cannot help it. While I am relieved to know that you do not steal for no reason, so much of your life is kept in secret. Have you never considered another career? I knew you would be angry, and that it is hardly a point of pride for me to intercede. But I have gone to my nephew, and enquired after a position for you. He needs a man of business to run his estates and prevent him from being as ninny-hammered as he was when he lost my house. And you are quite the smartest man I know.' She laid the sheet of parchment in front of him.

He glared up at her. 'You were enquiring after honest employment for me?'

'Yes, Tony.'

'Was there anything in our brief interaction that led you to believe that I might welcome a change of career?'

'Well, no, Tony.'

'And did I not specifically request that you never trouble me on the subject, and tell you that I had no intention to change for you or any other?'

She stared at the floor. She had promised. She had sworn to him that it would not matter, and, by asking, she was forswearing herself. She raised her chin to look into his eyes. 'I understand. I am sorry. It was not my place.'

He stared back at her and she felt her lip begin to tremble. She wished she could turn and run, and not say the rest of the words she would have to say, before this could be over. 'Tony.' She tried a small sip of the brandy, but it did nothing to improve her nerves.

He held out a hand for the paperwork. 'Do not look at me so. Give me the paper. I can at least read it, although I suspect you have heard my final answer on the subject.'

He took the papers away from her and sat back down at the desk, feet flat on the floor. Then he removed a pair of reading glasses from the pocket of his coat, brushed them absently against his lapel to clean them, and put them on. He leaned forward, resting his chin on his elbows, tossing his head to get the hair out of his eyes. 'No, no. This will never do. You'll have me counting sheep in the country for your half-witted nephew, so that you can have the comfort of knowing I lead a poor but honest life. It is not going to happen, no matter what your motives.'

And as she stared at him, the memory came flooding back to her. He had done the same in his house, and in hers, in chapel and in the library. She had always seen him thus, from the time he had learned to read, until she had left home and forgotten him. Anywhere that there was something to be read, she was liable to trip over him, polishing his spectacles and muttering over the paper. And some part of her mind assumed, should she go home, he would be there still, sitting under a tree in the garden, conjugating Latin and declaiming in Greek.

The brandy glass slipped from her hand and shattered on the desk. 'Eustace Smith.'

Without looking up he said, 'Connie, if you must insist on breaking the glassware, I'll leave you to explain it to Patrick. And I can assure you that I do not need menial employment, so you can take your offer with you. Or better yet, leave it and I will pass it on to my niece's new husband. Much more in his line, I think. He has a fine head on his shoulders, unlike your nephew the duke, and will soon have the estate put to right.'

'Eustace? It is you, isn't it?' She stood and planted her hands on the desk in front of him. 'Little Eustace Smith who used to live next door to me?'

When he looked up into her eyes, he was smiling, the smile of her lover, Tony Smythe. 'There was nothing little about me, even then.'

She swallowed hard at the memory of him.

'I have always been six months older than you, although you never noticed the fact. You were too busy dangling after my brothers, or the neighbours, or the duke.'

The words wounded her, for it made her feel like a fortune hunter, or, worse yet, the foolish young girl she had been.

'You were most interested in anyone else but me, as I remember it,' he reminded her.

Although the smile hid it, she could hear the pain in his voice, as though the wound was fresh. And perhaps it was, for she had been intimate with him, had loved him, and still not seen him for who he was.

'Oh, Eustace...' the name stuck on her tongue and she forced it out '...I am so sorry. So very sorry, not to have known it was you.'

He looked at her sharply. 'I have never favoured the name Eustace, nor has it favoured me.'

'But...but it is you, isn't it? To see you sitting there with your head in your hands, you are just as I remember you. Why didn't you say something?'

'So that I could listen to you dismiss me as "little Eustace"? Not a memory I needed to renew. Perhaps if you had recognised me. But there seemed to be no risk of that.'

She stared into his face as he peered at her from over his glasses and wondered how she could not have seen it. He looked very like his handsome older brothers.

She blushed to remember that she had been quite taken with the older Smiths. 'You do not wear your glasses any more?'

'I only ever needed them to read, and that was all I ever did, when you knew me last. Now I do so much of my work in the dark, glasses are really quite useless. It is easier to operate by touch.'

She blushed, remembering how good he was in the dark, when operating by touch. 'It was a very long time ago. And you are most different than you were.'

He sighed. 'And you are very much the same as I remember. Every bit as beautiful as when you left home. And still in search of a title. How goes the husband hunt?'

'Better than it had been, now that Barton is out of the way.' Her voice was a little tart. 'I have you to thank, for clearing the way for more honourable men.'

He looked tired. 'I would have removed Barton, in any case. But it pleases me you benefited from it.'

'So when you took the deed for me?'

'I was helping out an old friend.'

'And I am just an old friend to you?'

He looked at her long and hard. 'If that is what you wish. But I suspect that you came here for a matter more personal than friendship. Enough nonsense, Connie. I was right in my surmise, was I not? You were not to blame for the barren union at all.'

She shook her head.

'Have you come to torment me with the knowledge that by removing Barton, I have helped clear the path for some other man? Or do you need me, again? Have you come as you promised to? Come, out with it. What is the truth?'

She nodded. She needed him again, to fix yet another problem. He must be terribly tired of women in distress to look after and change one's plans for. He had just got free of his sisters, and now he would be saddled with her. And when she opened her mouth to speak, she sobbed.

He rose from behind the desk quickly and caught her in his arms. 'I am sorry that I spoiled your plans to catch another peer. I know you do not want me, and that I am not nearly good enough for you.' His voice was rough. 'But if you are carrying my child, I really must insist.' He swallowed, and when he spoke his tone was strong and confident again. 'Let me take care of you.'

'No.'

He stiffened against her.

'I am honoured that you will have me. But I am so sorry, Tony. So very, very sorry. I do not want you to have to take care of me, yet again. It is not fair to you, to never have what you want, but to have your future forced upon you by a foolish woman. Once you have married me, you need hardly take care of me at all. I will not be a bother. And I will do my best to take care of you.' She erupted in a fresh bout of tears.

'There now, do not cry.'

'I cannot help it. I cry at every little thing, I am sick in the morning, tired during the day, restless at night.' She sobbed into the wool of his coat. 'And I was afraid to come here, but afraid to stay away.'

'You have nothing to be afraid of, any more.' He was stroking her hair and holding her tight against him. 'Everything will be all right, if you will just say yes to me. Everything. I promise.'

'You warned me this would happen. But I wanted you, and I wanted a baby as well, no matter the consequences. And then I forgot all about the risks and wanted to feel what I felt whenever I was with you. I did not think what it might be like for the poor baby to have such a fool for a mother, or care that you would not want to marry.'

'When did I ever say that?'

'You said you loved elsewhere. And you would marry me for the sake of the child. I have been in such a marriage, Tony, and do not want another.'

'Were you so unhappy with the duke?' His voice was strange in her ear, shaky and hoarse. 'I always told myself that you were happy, and had what was best for you. And that I needn't concern myself.'

'After a fashion. I was fond of him, and he of me. We did comfortably together. And I did not love him, so it did not hurt so very much when he grew bored with me and visited with other women.'

'My poor darling.' He stroked her hair again.

'Now you will marry me, because you promised to. And I will be happy. I have always wanted children. Always. I will be very happy. And I will be a good mother, and a good wife to you.

'But some day you will say you are going to your club, but you will not come home. And I will lie alone in my bed, knowing that you have gone to her, and because I love you, but you can love only one woman, I fear it will break my heart.' She let loose with a fresh batch of tears.

He wrapped his arms even tighter around her, and waited for the sobbing to abate, passing her his handkerchief. 'You love me that much, do you?'

'Mnnnhmmm.'

'And you sent me away because…'

'It was foolish of me to fall in love with you. I could not keep you, and I could not control myself when you held me in your arms. I only ever felt alive when I was with you. The longer I kept you, the more I wanted you, and the more disgracefully I would behave to keep you with me, and the harder it would be to let you go. And it was already too late.'

The tears were ready to start again, but before they could, he kissed her and, for a moment, she forgot what it was that she was crying about.

'There, now. No more tears. Lay your head on my other shoulder where it is dry and comfortable, for the coat on the right is cried through to the shirt front.' He kissed her temple. 'Better?'

She nodded.

'Then I have a riddle. If I loved one woman my whole life, which is as long as I've known you, but she would look right through me if she saw me on the street, and she is as lovely and as far above me and unattainable as you are yourself, and I have kept myself apart from matrimony, until now, hoping for a miracle, can you not guess the identity of my great undying passion, the love of my life, the woman I would brave oceans and fight lions, and crawl in and out of three-storey windows to steal deeds for?'

She held very still, hoping he would just tell her what she wanted to hear. It couldn't be. But it must be, for he would never tease her so, if it weren't.

'And yet I was terrified to tell you the truth. I could not speak to you when we were children, and I could not speak to you now. There was only ever room in my heart for you, Constance. But if fate had not forced my hand, I might have been fool enough to let you marry someone else.'

She laid her hand on his arm and whispered. 'Do not think of it, again. Now that I have found you, there can be no other man for me, Anthony Smythe.' She furrowed her brow. It was not his true name, though she would always think of him thus. She tried again. 'I mean, Eu—'

He winced and covered her mouth with his fingers. 'Connie? Before you speak, let me warn you that it will spoil a lifetime of fantasy if you ever again call me by my given name. I did not take you to bed wishing to make you cry "oh, Eustace" loudly enough for the neighbours to hear.'

He had called her Connie. No one called her Connie any more. Not even Robert. But to her true friends she had always been Connie. She snuggled into the warmth of his shoulder, feeling safe, and it made her smile.

'If we have a boy, I'll hear no nonsense of naming him after his father. My mother fought to defend my brothers from that fate, but when it came to me, she no longer cared to be bothered, and let my father christen me Eustace Anthony after himself.'

'We will name him Anthony,' she murmured. 'After his father. It is a wonderful name. I am quite fond of it.'

'Very good.' He reached behind her knees and scooped her up into his arms. 'And now we will adjourn to the bedroom, where you can tell me that bit again, about how losing me would break your heart. Not that you ever will, of course.

'And perhaps later, we might go to Bond Street and choose a ring fitting worthy of a former duchess.'

'You needn't, really,' she whispered. 'Money is not important. If you truly love me.'

He laughed. 'I know, darling. And I would be only too happy to live on love, if I have you. But what shall

I do with the great stacks of money that I got off Barton? The safe did not contain what I was looking for, but it was full to the top with hundred-pound notes. Why did the fool want to print his own money, when he had a safe full of the stuff?' He shrugged. 'If he did not appreciate his wealth, I saw no reason to let him keep it.'

'You thief,' she said. But she was laughing.

And she raised her face to his, and let him steal another kiss.

On sale 1st February 2008

THE UNWILLING BRIDE
by Margaret Moore

Promised to Merrick of Tregellas when she was but
a child, Lady Constance was unwilling to wed a man she
remembered only as a spoiled boy. Convinced he had
grown into an arrogant knight, she sought to make
herself so unappealing that Merrick would refuse to
honour their betrothal.

Yet no sooner had this enigmatic, darkly handsome
man ridden through the castle gates than she
realised he was nothing like the boy she recalled.
And very much a man she could love...

Celebrate 100 years of pure reading pleasure with Mills & Boon®

To mark our centenary, each month we're
publishing a special 100th Birthday Edition.
These celebratory editions are packed with extra
features and include a FREE bonus story.

Now that's worth celebrating!

4th January 2008

The Vanishing Viscountess by Diane Gaston
With FREE story The Mysterious Miss M
*This award-winning tale of the Regency Underworld
launched Diane Gaston's writing career.*

1st February 2008

Cattle Rancher, Secret Son by Margaret Way
With FREE story His Heiress Wife
Margaret Way excels at rugged Outback heroes...

15th February 2008

Raintree: Inferno by Linda Howard
With FREE story Loving Evangeline
*A double dose of Linda Howard's heady mix of
passion and adventure.*

Don't miss out! From February you'll have the
chance to enter our fabulous monthly prize draw.
See special 100th Birthday Editions for details.

www.millsandboon.co.uk

2 FREE

BOOKS AND A SURPRISE GIFT!

We would like to take this opportunity to thank you for reading this Mills & Boon® book by offering you the chance to take TWO more specially selected titles from the Historical series absolutely FREE! We're also making this offer to introduce you to the benefits of the Mills & Boon® Reader Service™—

- ★ **FREE home delivery**
- ★ **FREE gifts and competitions**
- ★ **FREE monthly Newsletter**
- ★ **Exclusive Reader Service offers**
- ★ **Books available before they're in the shops**

Accepting these FREE books and gift places you under no obligation to buy, you may cancel at any time, even after receiving your free shipment. Simply complete your details below and return the entire page to the address below. You don't even need a stamp!

YES! Please send me 2 free Historical books and a surprise gift. I understand that unless you hear from me, I will receive 4 superb new titles every month for just £3.69 each, postage and packing free. I am under no obligation to purchase any books and may cancel my subscription at any time. The free books and gift will be mine to keep in any case.

H8ZED

Ms/Mrs/Miss/Mr ....Initials ....
BLOCK CAPITALS PLEASE

Surname ....

Address ....

....

....Postcode..............................

Send this whole page to:
UK: FREEPOST CN81, Croydon, CR9 3WZ